J. Kent Messum is an author, musician and always bets on the underdog. He lives in Toronto with his wife, dog and a trio of cats.

PENGUIN BOOKS

Bait

Bait

J. KENT MESSUM

PENGUIN BOOKS

PENGUIN BOOKS

Published by the Penguin Group
Penguin Books Ltd, 80 Strand, London WC2R ORL, England
Penguin Group (USA) Inc., 375 Hudson Street, New York, New York 10014, USA
Penguin Group (Canada), 90 Eglinton Avenue East, Suite 700, Toronto, Ontario, Canada M4P 2Y3
(a division of Pearson Penguin Canada Inc.)
Penguin Ireland, 25 St Stephen's Green, Dublin 2, Ireland (a division of Penguin Books Ltd)
Penguin Group (Australia), 707 Collins Street, Melbourne, Victoria 3008, Australia
(a division of Pearson Australia Group Pty Ltd)
Penguin Books India Pvt Ltd, 11 Community Centre, Panchsheel Park, New Delhi – 110 017, India
Penguin Group (NZ), 67 Apollo Drive, Rosedale, Auckland 0632, New Zealand
(a division of Pearson New Zealand Ltd)
Penguin Books (South Africa) (Pty) Ltd, Block D, Rosebank Office Park,
181 Jan Smuts Avenue, Parktown North, Gauteng 2193, South Africa

Penguin Books Ltd, Registered Offices: 80 Strand, London WC2R ORL, England

www.penguin.com

First published in the United States of America by Plume,
a division of Penguin Group (USA) Inc., 2013
First published in Great Britain in Penguin Books 2013
001

Typeset by Penguin Books Ltd
Printed in Great Britain by Clays Ltd, St Ives plc

A CIP catalogue record for this book is available from the British Library

ISBN: 978–1–405–91424–6

www.greenpenguin.co.uk

For Kara

Prologue

SIX MONTHS AGO.

Tick McCabe was sure he could make it. The shore seemed maddeningly close. Less than a hundred yards to go and he still had the strength to continue despite everything he'd endured. The same couldn't be said for the others. Their luck had run out. Several minutes had passed since Tick heard the last of their waterlogged screams.

Screw them, he thought. *All the more for me.*

He picked out a large rock on the beach and aimed for it, front-crawling with all the energy he could muster. Progress seemed slow. His body was maxed, sore arms chopping waves, stiff legs scissoring, overworked lungs whistling for air. Cold water pressed inside his ear canals as salt stung his eyes.

Almost there. Keep your eyes on the prize.

1

From behind him the sounds of laughter rang out. Hoots and jeers working to undermine his confidence. Between splashing and breathing he could hear the taunts clearly, telling him everything he didn't want to know. Tick turned over to do the back crawl, hitching in a chest full of air.

"Burn in hell, you sons of bitches!"

He expected a barrage of insults, but the howls ceased. Instead there was a lull, voices oddly pacified. Then a clamor arose and something large and rough bumped into Tick's side, rocking him in the water, making him scream out. An indistinct mass of blue and gray stripes broke the surface and filled the corner of his eye, only to be gone the next instant. Tick treaded water, frantically sweeping glances over the waves. The big one had struck him that time. He was sure of it.

"Shit, shit, shit."

It was the third bump Tick had taken in the water. This one had been harder and more confident than the others. Probably the last inquisitive hit he would get. Once curiosity was satisfied, Tick would undoubtedly be taken under.

So close.

His front crawl became more desperate. He needed more time, maybe two or three minutes. If only he was allowed to have *that* of all things. The irony left a bitter taste in his mouth. Tick had lived most of his life with nothing but time on his hands. Now he had precious little, sucked dry in the last few days, which had seen him living more and more on borrowed amounts.

Almost there.

He tried to occupy his mind with anything that would keep it from focusing on what was in the water with him. Muddled memories and half-truths distracted him a little, so many regrets, too many mistakes. If he'd listened, if he'd taken a left over right at a fork in the road, if he hadn't been so damned hung up and strung out all the time, maybe things would have turned out different.

Stop it. Focus. You can do this. Your life depends on it.

Tick couldn't focus. Twenty-seven years of age and half of that misspent. Rock bottom had been his status for a while now. His existence felt like it could be nothing else. There was no other way but further down, his failing body heavy, sinking under the scar tissue of an irreparably damaged life. Even the people he thought closest to him were distant. They called him *Tick*, after all. He was little more than lice to them.

Not far now.

Fuck Tick. Gerald was his name. Gerald Francis McCabe. He couldn't get that out of his head. The full, proper name suddenly seemed important, key to his corporality. It was his original self, a true identity from long ago, the name his mother and father called him, the name that his siblings, friends, and lovers used. How long had it been since he'd spoken to anyone who called him by name?

Almost—

Something grabbed his right foot and pulled downward. Tick went under, taking a mouthful of salt water, refusing to open his eyes as a force shook him violently below the surface. He fought hard, shaking and twisting his leg against the ferocious grip. Kicking out with his other foot, he connected with something that didn't like being hit. With one more savage shake there was a pop and release, freedom coming at a painful price. Tick broke the surface with a gasp. Sounds of nearby laughter stabbed at him. He tried to continue swimming, but his right leg didn't seem as effective as before. A trail of maroon spread behind him as he kicked and stroked. Gray and white shapes writhed through the discoloration. Tick turned onto his back and raised his right leg out of the water.

"Oh, God," he croaked.

His foot was gone. What remained was a torn stump, flap of skin flopping against ripped meat under the gleam of bone. Sea salt burned the wound. Tick wailed with so much despair he almost choked on it.

"Oh, Jesus, oh, Christ. Just another minute. That's all I needed. Just one more goddamn—"

Again he went under, pulled by the other foot. He fought again to free himself, hammering painfully at that which gripped him with his new stump. In no time his left foot was separated from his body. He opened his eyes and saw every blurred color and shape he wished was not there. The most solid of these began to converge on him.

Gerald Francis McCabe, he thought. *That's who I was—*

He was struck from every angle and with every measure of force. Blood bloomed thick around him. Tick did not resurface. Nearby, beer bottles clinked, cigars burned, and significant money exchanged hands.

Part One

JONESING

One

NOW.

hat an incredible dream.

Small waves hitting the beach, the cry of gulls, the baking heat on his face. All of it should have convinced him otherwise, yet he was certain it was all part of some vivid dream. The press of sun through his eyelids brightened his blackout, though he could not awaken. Trapped in the twilight of emerging thought, he could feel the weight of his body pressing into sand. A cool breeze rippled clothes and licked his hair. Fresh air filled his lungs, the smell of salt water dancing in his nostrils. Goose bumps rose on his forearms as grains of sand peppered him. The clarity of it all was astounding, absolutely electrifying. The good stuff had taken him to wondrous dreamscapes before, but never this real. Not even close.

Might be my best high yet.

Then it dawned on him that there was a difference at the center of this chimera, a horrible absence of euphoria that couldn't be attributed to the devil's dust. The hollowness he felt unnerved him. Nash Lemont was now full of doubt. Where was the worm inside his head?

This isn't a dream.

Increasing clarity eroded his remaining slumber. Any similarities to dreams broke away in pieces like an eggshell, leaving soft-boiled sobriety underneath. The components of Nash's body came sluggishly back to life. Feet kicked out for the feel of a mattress. Hands grasped for bedsheets. Ears strained for the sounds of city life. Eyelids cracked open, only to squint at the sun's glare.

Nash rolled over and shook the grogginess from his head, coughing up phlegm, red-rimmed eyes straining open. He could define little. Wide blurs of blue and white streaked with shades of brown and green stretched before him. In the center of his vision sat a drab figure with slumped shoulders.

"Shit, you look like I feel," a high voice informed him.

"Huh?"

Nash propped himself up on his elbows, blinking to clear his sight. He peered again at the figure, trying to focus. The figure shifted and hunched. It was slender with white, dirty skin. Long thick hair hung over the face. The hidden features and gargoyle posture made

Nash uncomfortable. He wiped away sand stuck to his sweating cheek and looked around in a hundred-and-eighty-degree sweep. What came from his mouth was little more than a croak.

"Where . . . ?"

From his ten to two o'clock a wall of tall grass made a natural fence along the shore. He ran his line of sight down the green divider until he reached his three o'clock. What he saw there made him gasp. The unexpected white beach did not alarm Nash Lemont. What alarmed Nash was the other bodies flopped on the sand.

Two

THREE DAYS AGO.

What alarmed Nash was how much no-name-brand shit he was putting into his grocery basket these days. There was a time, and not too long ago, when he would have insisted on some brand names among his purchases. Some things you just didn't crap out on: ketchup, mustard, mayo, mac 'n' cheese, margarine maybe. Now all he looked for was the cheapest alternative, willing to undercut any provision he once enjoyed with its poorer, dumber cousin. Nash picked up a bottle of ketchup.

"Heinz," he said, looking at the label. "There are no other kinds."

But there were other kinds, for less than half the price too. Their names were suspect—he'd never even remotely heard of them. Some had writing on the labels in languages Nash had never seen.

Some Middle Eastern or Indonesian crap or something, he thought as he dropped one in the basket.

These shopping trips were where Nash felt most pathetic. Budget stretched so thin it was floss compared to the kind of money he'd dropped once upon a time. His eyes moistened as the full realization of his situation sank in once again. He looked at the discount peanut butter brands, gritty and oily, reserved for the poor.

"Rock bottom," he mumbled.

So unbelievably *broke* all the time, that was what he was. When he was lucky enough to get some money it couldn't stay in his wallet for more than a few hours before he pissed it away or blew it up his arm. The more he thought about it the shittier he felt. Shame coated the bottom of his belly in lead and cramped the smooth muscle around his heart. Nine out of ten addicts never recover. Nash never liked those odds.

The aisles weren't busy. He strolled, taking advantage of the supermarket's air-conditioning, a luxury he no longer enjoyed in his apartment due to his need for some fast cash. It was nice to get out of the hot Miami sun. Midday was a real bitch, even for your well-tanned types. Nash checked his watch, only to find it missing as well. A moment of confusion before the penny dropped.

He'd sold that too, to his superintendent, for a measly ten bucks.

Nash grabbed a jar of kosher dills and found himself inspecting his fingers instead of the pickles. They looked worn and leathery, flesh so dull it barely passed for pink. One of his thumbnails was a purplish black. Knuckles were scabbed too. Nash pressed on the discolored nail with the tip of his index. Throbs of pain drummed his nerve endings.

Did I shut that in a door or something? he thought, trying hard to remember. *Did I deck someone?*

No recollection. He replaced the jar on the shelf and that was when he caught the man looking. At the end of the aisle, standing in front of the shelves of canned soup, some dude was thoroughly checking him out. Nash scowled. The man turned his face away, void of expression.

"Not your type, fag," Nash muttered, making a U-turn.

He found himself in the frozen food section, overly eyeing the tanned legs and cutoff shorts of a college coed to reaffirm his heterosexuality. She was tight and sweet, midriff bared and topped with a couple of candy apple tits in a tube top. Despite the sex appeal, she still had an air of innocence about her, as if she'd only accommodated a cock or two in her young life. That was the kind of girl Nash liked most, the almost-virgins, the ones you still had to show the ropes, toss around the bedroom a bit. He waited impatiently for his dick to chub in his pants. The erection never came.

Pick up some Viagra with my next order, he thought. *Try Pablo, he might have some kicking around.*

The girl felt Nash's eyes on her and slipped away, leaving him staring at a stack of pizzas through a glass freezer door. He only had twenty bucks to spend on food for the week. His basket contained mostly instant noodles and canned soup. There were some oranges and carrots in there too: an oddity among the other goods, but a new necessity for Nash. A few weeks ago his pal Roon complained to a clinic nurse that his teeth felt like they were rotating in his gums. Turned out he'd come down with a case of scurvy due to the fact that he hadn't eaten a fresh fruit or vegetable in months. Nash couldn't remember the last time he had eaten anything nutritious either.

He wandered the frosted windows, perusing the microwave dinners and desserts. Most weren't afford-able, so Nash returned to the aisle of cheap shit where his admirer had been earlier, only to find him gone. He breathed a sigh of relief, dumped three cans of tuna into his basket, and headed for the checkout. As he joined the express line he made plans to swing a discount on his next score by offering one of his old acoustic guitars as collateral. That was when he noticed his admirer, still in the supermarket and still interested.

The guy stood in another line a few checkouts over, watching intently and holding a carton of milk. They made eye contact for three long seconds as Nash took in his details this time: crew cut, clean shaven, unfriendly manner, not an ounce of fat on the guy. There was a militant sense about him that Nash couldn't ignore.

Narc, Nash thought. *Fuck.*

Nash was carrying. Not much, but enough on top of his existing record to get him put away in the realm of years, not months. The lady ahead of him paid for her groceries and left. Nash was being rung through. The double door exit was less than twenty yards to his right. He thought about making a run for it.

Not the front. They'll have that covered.

Nash put his basket down on the conveyer belt and rolled his eyes.

"Jeez, I forgot milk," he said to the checkout girl. "I'll just grab it quick. It's at the back, right?"

The checkout girl said nothing, only fluttered purple eyelids and chewed gum.

"Just gimme one sec."

He moved quickly, past the line, down the aisle to the rear of the supermarket. A sign reading *Employees Only* on a metal door with a honeycombed porthole caught his attention. He breached it without a second thought, hearing a stock boy yell out after him for his violation. Nash was through the loading bay and out an emergency exit in seconds.

Don't stop for one second, he thought. *Don't even dare.*

Nash scrambled up the alleyway, dodging skids and jumping boxes, throwing glances over his shoulder the whole way. A panic he had not known before this day enveloped him.

Three

NOW.

Nash scrambled to his feet in a panic, kicking sand out from underneath him. The bodies of two men and a woman lay motionless before his eyes. One man was black, the other white, the woman Hispanic if Nash wasn't mistaken. He assumed they were dead, but soon saw their stomachs rise and fall with breath.

"They're alive," the squatted figure behind him said. "Don't know what good it's gonna do us, though."

The voice seemed dry and distant, the sound of a message crackling through a megaphone from a city block away. Nash ignored it and took the time to inspect his strange new environment. Wherever he was, he hadn't the slightest idea how he'd come to be there or why.

". . . the hell is going on?" he asked aloud, wiping sweat and sand from his face.

The figure said nothing. Nash racked his brain. It relinquished little. He couldn't even remember the last time he had been on a beach. The capacity to recall things easily was gone. One of his lifestyle's many side effects was the deletion of brain cells and Nash had been subtracting for some time now. Every memory lacked depth and detail.

"Where . . . ?"

The shock of his surroundings, the confusion, it was almost too much. He felt light-headed, the muscles in his face going soft, a bubble of watery vomit catching in his throat. Hands clasped behind his head, fingers pulling hair, Nash hissed with pain as he fought to stay focused.

"What . . . what are we doing here?"

Nash threw his head back and breathed deep to try to offset the panic pushing inside his chest. The sun was hot and high in the sky, suggesting noon. The figure began to rock on its haunches, drawing Nash's attention. Its movements were compulsive, unhinged, suggestive of a mental patient or victim in shock. Nash feared both.

"Who are you?" he asked, taking a step back.

The figure snorted and spat. It flew like a bullet, making a dent in the sand. Nash took it as a warning shot, but cared little. He challenged with his own gob, planting it between them.

"You got a name?"

He considered tagging *bitch* onto his question, but decided against it. Puffing chests felt premature, and judging by the situation so far, he thought it unwise to make enemies. It was becoming clear that the squatting figure was a woman, albeit an ugly one. The high voice implied a chick, but the fearlessness in the tone made Nash unsure. He looked closer and saw the curve of breast under her dirty Harley-Davidson T-shirt. She examined a clump of tangled hair hanging in her face and didn't reply. Nash raised his voice.

"Hey, I'm talking to you."

Phlegm rattled in the woman's throat and she spat with more menace, this time in Nash's direction, the gob missing him by a foot.

"Name's Nunya," the woman said.

"Nunya?"

Nash knew he'd stepped in it as soon as the word left his lips. He rolled his eyes before she replied. He'd used this one himself countless times.

"Yeah, Nunya fucking business."

Nash laughed. He didn't know why. The woman turned and regarded him with a scowl. Nash stopped laughing at the sight of her. Calling her ugly was a mistake. She might have been a looker if she bothered to clean herself up. Disheveled, reddish-brown hair hung in near dreadlocks alongside her dirty face. She looked battle scarred, war weary; ripe for early retirement. Nash's tongue perused a few gaps in his teeth, reminding him that he was no spring chicken either.

"Well, pleased to meet you, Nunya," he said with a smirk. "I'm Nash."

She let out a haughty breath at the introduction and turned away. She was in no mood for pleasantries, evidenced by her third spit in as many minutes.

"Ah, Christ, man," she said. "I'm not having you call me that for the rest of whatever. My name's Ginger. Don't forget it. I ain't telling you again."

Nash was sure he could remember. "Ginger. Okay, got it. Is that a nickname or something?"

Ginger leaned back and stretched out on the sand, already tired of his questions. Behind her, Nash noticed a set of footprints trailing off into the brush. There was at least one more person around.

What have we gotten ourselves into? he thought.

He looked back at the three unconscious bodies. They all looked like inner-city trash: worn clothes and bad complexions. Nothing respectable about any of them and no question they were all from the same bracket of society. The one found around the rim of Miami's asshole.

I wonder who the worst of this bunch is. . . .

The worst what, Nash wasn't even sure. Ginger

scratched her arm savagely. The action cued Nash to do the same. The itching was just beginning.

"Don't suppose you got a clue about any of this?" Nash asked.

Ginger sat back up, flinging dreadlocks out of her face, thin frame rigid with attitude. She simply stared at him. Nash's annoyance grew at her lack of an answer.

"What the fuck is happening here?"

Ginger shrugged nonchalantly. The smile she gave was surprisingly sweet and might have fooled others, but Nash caught wind of the bullshit behind it. He recognized her type, little liar playing mind games. Nash had banged broads like her throughout his music career: aspiring actresses and singers with habits to feed, wading into the party scene, hoping to suck or fuck for a foot in the door before fading away or burning out.

"Maybe we're sweepstakes winners," she said finally.

Nash sighed. "You got no idea, do you?"

He gave her his most unimpressed look, but she didn't notice. She couldn't have been less interested in him or his opinion of her. Instead, she turned to face the ocean, closing her eyes to the breeze that came off the water and brushed her cheeks.

"Honestly, I don't have a clue, cowboy . . . unless this is some messed-up reality TV show, or *Candid Camera* on crack."

The thought suddenly seemed plausible in lieu of any other explanation. Nash scanned the bushes and trees, searching for a hidden camera lens among the leaves or a boom mic among the branches.

"Of course, I'm gonna beat the living shit out of the host when they unveil themselves," Ginger continued. "We'll see how much TV personality they have after I ram a whole camera crew up their ass."

Her volume was enough to awaken the black man. He stirred and grunted, fingers raking the sand. His skin was the color of coal, a graying goatee prominent on his tired face. Muscular arms and shoulders implied a well-kept physique, but his unbuttoned shirt revealed a bloated belly. The man awakened slowly, painfully. He rolled over and rose with his back to them, shaking sand from his salt-and-pepper dreadlocks. Nash figured the guy was well past forty.

"Wakey, wakey," Nash said. "Rise and shine."

The man spun at the sound of his voice. His posture became defensive, beady brown eyes darting between Nash and Ginger, hands balling into fists and rising to strike.

"It's alright, man," Nash assured him, his own hands held out in a calming gesture. "Take it easy now. We're just as confused as you are."

The man's wary eyes stayed on them while he patted down the pockets of his cargo shorts. Nash realized that he hadn't checked his own pockets and copied. Everything that should have been there was missing. Ginger smirked at both of them.

"You won't find anything," she cawed. "I already searched the lot of you."

The man shot her a cold look. "So your hands found their way into my pants already, huh?"

She waved a middle finger. "Get bent."

The man returned the gesture, backing up until he was satisfied with the distance. A look of worry flashed across his face, gone as quickly as it had come, but Nash took note. The man needed something, a fact, an answer, a truth he could use as a starting point, but he looked too proud, too resilient to ask anyone for a favor. Nash knew exactly how he felt. He offered to get the ball rolling.

"Name's Nash. What's yours?"

The man didn't answer. Instead he checked around, head movements twitchy with something akin to a nervous tic as he gathered all he could from his surroundings. When he wasn't satisfied he turned back with knitted eyebrows and head cocked in question.

"Hell if I know, pal," Nash replied.

The man nodded as if he fully understood. Nash got the impression that this cat woke up in random places on a regular basis. He swung a pointed finger over to Ginger by way of introduction.

"That's Ginger. We just met."

"What about the others over there?" the man asked, thumbing to the last two unconscious bodies. "Who they?"

"No idea. They've been out cold since we woke up. I've never seen them before in my life."

The man analyzed the other man lying facedown in the sand, obviously the youngest among them, just a kid, really, probably not even legal drinking age. The Hispanic woman looked a few years older.

"Your name?" Nash asked again.

The man let out a rumbling cough to clear his throat and composed himself a little. When he spoke his voice took on new depth and grit.

"Felix is the name. Looks like we got us one more?"

He jabbed his goatee toward the trail of footprints leading away from them. Ginger said nothing. Nash shrugged.

"I guess so, but I haven't seen anyone else. I woke up not long before you did."

Nash paused, expecting Ginger to add something to the conversation. She seemed about as interested in talking as getting off her ass. Nash shrugged again.

"Wish I could tell you more."

He walked down to the water's edge and let the small waves rush around the soles of his worn sneakers, sinking his heels back into the sand as they retreated. An awkward silence descended.

"Are we on an island?" Felix finally asked.

"Don't know."

Nash scanned the beach and vegetation and realized they likely inhabited very little landmass. He felt stupid. He hadn't even thought to ask important questions. Felix wasn't impressed.

"How'd we get here?"

"Don't know."

"Well, what do you know?"

Nash chewed his bottom lip and said nothing. Felix waited impatiently, his agitation growing. He finally turned his back and shook his head.

"Fucking crackers," he said. "All y'all never know shit about shit."

"Oh, fuck you, Sambo," Nash spat. "I'm sure you know less than I do."

Felix glared at him. "Call me that again, motherfucker. I dare you."

Nash drew in breath as Felix's fists clenched and readied. Ginger's squeal of laughter ended everything before it began.

"Oh, yeah, we're gonna get along just fine."

Four

TWO DAYS AGO.

"**S**ure, we'll get along fine."

Ginger Rosen realized she was talking aloud as she sat on the cold toilet and squeezed out a half pint. The speech she had been practicing over and over in her head had grown angrier and was now working her mouth as well as her brain. Curtis was dreaming if he thought she'd be up for his little suggestion. Sarcasm coated her words before she spat them out.

"We'll all get along like a frigging house on fire."

Things between her and Curtis had been going from bad to worse, and now his demand for a threesome, with that bitch Rita no less, was her cue to start forming an exit strategy. Despite Curtis's assurances that they could all play nice, the idea of sharing a squeaky bed with one of his skank associates made Ginger's skin crawl. God knew what STDs Rita was carrying. Ginger didn't need any more complications in her life, and certainly none of that variety. Her past scrapes with the clap were more than enough. What Ginger needed was a distraction. The poster plastered to the inside of the stall door screamed at her in fiery orange graffiti:

Fuel Injector Live @ The Barracuda Room
10pm show. $5 cover. Ladies free!

There was a photo of the band below. The members looked well past their prime, posing against a brick wall under the misguided impression that they were in any way still cool or relevant. She thought about tearing the poster down and wiping her cooch with it. When she found no toilet paper in the dispenser, she did.

"Fucking dump," she muttered as she elbowed open the stall door. "Why do I keep coming back here?"

Her mind was a reflex. *Because it's one of the only bridges left that you haven't burned yet.*

Ginger went to the bathroom mirror and looked at the reflection of a woman who wasn't allowed in very many local establishments anymore. A single long crack down the middle of the glass refracted her slim body, making her appear even thinner. Greasy streaks on the surface smeared her features. Bloodshot eyes were returning to normal, though she still felt a little high. There was a residual paranoia that she could never shake after smoking the hash she pilfered from Curtis's stash, something she planned to bury soon under a much stronger score, if she was lucky.

Ginger shook out her hair and undid another button on her shirt, letting her cleavage pop more. Her perfect C-cups had aided and abetted her for as long as she could remember, though judging by the space for rent inside her bra these days, her tits had shrunk to a B. Her previous kind of pull had shrunk with them. She reapplied lipstick and touched up her mascara until she was sure she'd attained that fuckable look that always seemed to bring boons from others.

She walked out to the bar. Still early, but the Barracuda Room was starting to get busy, despite its notoriety as a dive. A stale, sour smell hung in the air. The sticky floor hadn't been washed in weeks. An overabundance of neon beer and liquor signs on the walls served as the only decorations. Her stool at the end of the bar was still vacant. Jojo the bartender was good about keeping it free of other customers. Ginger sat and he had a vodka-cran in front of her before she even opened her mouth.

"Thanks, handsome."

Jojo winked. "I know what my girl likes."

Ginger was nobody's girl, but she winked back

nonetheless. It was a half joke coming from him, but she knew he'd bang her in a New York minute if she ever gave the green light. Tickling his fancy just enough kept the odd free drink coming. She conceded Jojo was cute, extra points for putting up with her bad nights and occasional temper, but he was not her type. No one was her type. If she ever got too hard up, however, she knew the bartender would pay one way or another to bed her. She kept that opportunity simmering on the back burner, knowing her impending bust-up with Curtis would leave her in need of both cock and cash. Ginger batted eyelashes at Jojo as he snuck another look at her cleavage.

"If you could see me now, Curtis . . ." she mumbled.

Curtis Moffat, her unfaithful partner of two years, no doubt cooking up a spoon with Rita in some motel room right about now, would find his ass dumped by the end of the week. It was a good thing. Ginger didn't like what he was getting into nowadays. When she first hooked up with him he'd only dealt pot and prescription pills. It wasn't long before he graduated to coke and smack, but more recently he'd been running guns. She didn't want to know what else he might be involved in.

Ginger sipped her drink and scanned the room for prospects. Slim pickings, hardly worth a second glance, but one person managed to catch her eye. A man, and maybe a bit of a looker, stared at her from the gloom behind the pool tables at the back. She held his gaze long enough to suggest invitation.

Game on, she thought.

He didn't move, just sipped his Corona and kept staring, not even coy about it. Ginger looked away, pretending to be interested in the selection of bottles on the bar racks. When she looked back his eyes were still fixed. She felt the intensity from across the room.

Been a while, sailor?

And a sailor he might be. He looked the part: clean shaven, dark hair in a buzz cut, trim figure, and nice clothes. So completely out of place, Ginger could only assume he was in port for the week with some shore leave. She hoped he had some cash to burn and a sweet tooth for a fix, hard candy or better. She took an ice cube in with a gulp of cocktail and crunched it, raising an eyebrow at her new fan's improper stare.

"You think I'm gonna come to you, bub?" she muttered.

The man seemed to hear that. He took another sip of beer and began making his way over, sidestepping the clubgoers between them. Ginger looked away again and counted down the seconds in her head until his arrival.

Six, five, four, three, two—

"Hello there, gorgeous."

She turned. He was a little older than she'd originally

thought, but better looking up close and out of the shadows. The New York accent had its charm.

"Hi."

"You look thirsty. Can I buy you a drink?"

It was a terrible opener. Ginger almost walked. She reconsidered, eyeing his figure, taking note of his dimpled chin and strong hands. It wasn't every day that such hotness offered to buy her a round. She resolved to give him a three-strike limit.

"As soon as I finish this one you can," she replied, taking another sip.

He chuckled. "So, what's a girl like you doing in a joint like this?"

Not much better. Ginger thought it was she who should be asking him that question. She was right at home in the Barracuda Room. He looked like he had the wrong address.

"Is there somewhere better I should be?"

The man grinned. "Maybe."

Ginger played it so cool it might have come off frigid, but she took the straw out of her drink and nibbled the end to give him a preview of her mouth at work.

"You got something in mind, sailor?"

"That depends."

"And on what does it depend?"

The man paused, checked over his shoulder, leaned closer. The overapplication of aftershave was offensive, coming off of him like fumes, enough that if Ginger had been smoking they probably both would have gone up in flames.

"What are you into?" he asked, his tone lowering.

Ginger smirked. "What am I into? You kinky or something?"

The man's cheeks reddened. "No, I mean, I'm just wondering if you like to . . . um, if you like to *party*."

"I always like to party, baby."

"Well, I can hook you up if you wanna follow me outta here. Anything you want, anything at all. I got it."

"How much?"

"I'm sure we can work something out."

Ginger couldn't believe her luck. Excitement gripped her, but alarm followed quick on its heels. Ginger was used to the unusual, but this was getting uncomfortable as well. The guy and the speed at which the conversation was going didn't add up.

"Anything I want, you say?" she asked.

"Just name your poison."

She didn't like that, or the grin that followed. A particular memory suddenly struck her, that of an old acquaintance named Talia Wint, a working girl who had become a cautionary tale in the neighborhood. Eight months prior, Wint went missing from her corner for a week before her headless corpse wound up in a Dumpster. The body was a mess, according to the grapevine, so bad that people avoided discussing the details. The head never reappeared. Case still unsolved. Ginger looked over at Jojo, trying to get him to notice her new suitor, but he was too busy at the opposite end of the bar dealing with a pair of loudmouthed bitches.

"You've got a very pretty face," the man said.

That you might want to put on your mantel, she thought. "Aw, ain't you sweet."

"So, you wanna get out of here?"

"Easy, tiger, you got a name?"

His smile was sly. "Do I need one?"

Ginger returned the smile, but a shiver ran down her spine. She didn't like where this was going. Guy was too quick on the draw. It didn't look like he partied either, at least not at her level. She could tell he wasn't a dealer, a crook, or an addict who would be into her for the trade of sex for substance, despite his insinuations. Something else bothered her. The guy hadn't glanced down at her cleavage once.

"I'll take you up on that drink," she said and downed the rest of her vodka-cran.

"Mind if I make it a double?"

"Long as you make it tall too."

The man waved two fingers and Jojo came down the bar, happy to get away from the two squawkers doing shots at the other end.

"A Corona and another of what the lady is having, this time double and tall."

Jojo nodded and cast a sideways glance at Ginger, who made no sign that she was in need of assistance anymore. She planned to be out of there in a matter of minutes.

"Hey, stud, while my drink is being fixed I'm gonna go to the ladies', powder my nose and stuff."

"Don't you be gone too long, now."

Ginger giggled. "And miss out on you treating me right tonight? I think not. This stool better be free when I get back."

The man nodded. "I got it covered."

Ginger figured the drinks order would keep him anchored for long enough. She slipped off her stool and headed for the washroom, feeling him watch her the whole way, eyes slithering over her hips and ass as she walked. It wasn't lecherous. Predatory was the sense she got. She wanted to shed his gaze like a snakeskin. When she reached the washroom door she risked a glance over her shoulder. The man was distracted a moment, one of the two mouthy girls yelling at him about how cute he looked.

Good, she thought. *Cut the head of that bitch, buddy.*

Ginger took her chance and banked right, ducking behind a group of people who had just come through the front doors. Before she knew it she was out into the cool night air and flagging down a cab. She'd have to go to Curtis soon, unable to avoid it much longer. Curtis Moffat had what she needed. The cabbie gave her a once-over as she slipped into the back.

"Where to, lady?"

"Anywhere but here."

Five

NOW.

"Anywhere but here," Ginger said, looking skyward. "Christ, anywhere but stuck on an island, forced to watch this pathetic little cockfight."

"He started it," Nash whined.

"Little?" Felix grunted, grabbing his crotch. "Honey, if I dropped this cock of mine on your head, you'd think a grand piano had landed on your dome."

Ginger's eyes could have cut glass. "Buddy, if you've ever wanted to see your own dick and balls sailing bloody through the air, then I suggest you keep talking."

"Dyke," Felix growled.

"Prick."

Nearby, the kid on the sand stirred. Nash took a step away, unsure of this one. He looked pale and wiry, unstable even in his sleep. Felix stepped closer until he was almost on top of the kid. Nash watched from the corner of his eye, fearing he might receive a bitch-slap for his earlier slur if he didn't stay vigilant.

"He's waking," Nash said.

"No shit, Sherlock."

Felix pushed the kid's hip with a foot. The kid grunted and slurred something profane, drool seeping from the corner of his mouth. Felix paused a moment, then delivered a fierce kick to the kid's shin, snapping him awake with a screech.

"What the hell did you kick him for?" yelled Ginger.

The kid writhed drunkenly in the sand, panicky breaths popping in and out of his lungs as he tried to get his bearings. Felix stepped back to give him some space, but it didn't help.

"Get away from me!" squealed the kid.

He scrambled to his feet, kicking sand over the still unconscious girl beside him. The baggy jeans he wore inhibited his movements, making him appear clumsy as he staggered back. His stretched and torn wife-beater revealed a thin, hairless chest, peppered with acne. He flailed his arms effeminately at the others, his words coming in a lisping, blubbery babble.

"Wherethefuckwhothefuckwhatthefuck?"

Great, Nash thought. *Enter the mincing twink.*

Wide-eyed and near tears, the kid retreated to the edge of the long grass, where he picked up a fist-sized rock. He crouched to make himself a smaller target in case anyone decided to take a run at him.

"Who the hell are you guys?" he shouted, holding up the rock as if it were a live grenade.

Nash advanced slowly, arms outstretched and palms to the ground to show he was no threat. Felix swept right, trying to maintain a low profile, looking as if he was preparing to tackle the kid. It did not go unnoticed.

"You wanna get stoned? Just take another step then, man!"

The kid's arm rose, threatening to pitch the rock, keeping Felix at a safe distance. Ginger finally stood, wiping sand from her ass. She marched past the two men and approached the youngest addition to their fucked-up little family, coming close enough to unbalance him. He stumbled, the rock fumbling from his hands and landing in front of her. Ginger put a foot on it.

"Don't you come any closer, cunt!" the kid yelled. "I know karate!"

"Look, calm down. I just—"

"You best back the hell up, or I'll—"

"Hey, will you chill the fuck out already?"

Ginger's explosiveness caused the kid to jump back. He looked at her with surprise and maybe a new respect.

Ginger put her hands on her hips and tipped her head sideways, lips pursed wearily. The kid hung his head at the sight of it, embarrassment pinching his face.

"You finished being a drama queen?" asked Ginger, voice suddenly soothing.

The kid swallowed hard and breathed deep, trying to regain some composure. Ginger took another step toward him.

"Do you, in fact, know karate?" She chuckled.

"No" was the sullen reply.

"I didn't think so. What's your name, kid?"

"Kenneth . . . Kenny. My friends . . . they call me Kenny."

"Kenny, Kenny, Kenny," she cooed. "You're not in any danger from us, okay? My name's Ginger. That's Nash and Felix. We're just as lost as you are, babe. Wish I could give you some answers, but I can't. So take a deep breath and relax as much as you can. No one is here to harm you, okay?"

Ginger gave Felix a glare for the shin kicking. The look he gave back said he'd do it again. Nash took a step toward Kenny, but the boy flinched.

"Listen to the lady, kid. We won't hurt you. She's right about that much."

The kid nodded, but inched closer to Ginger for protection. She let him enter her comfort zone easily. Nash was taken aback by the woman's kindness toward this new one in their midst, concluding it was some kind of homo thing. She was a dyke, kid was a fag, and that united them. Nash resented it.

"Okay," Kenny said, breathing slower. "I'm cooling out."

Ginger nodded. "Good. That's real good. . . ."

A few more words softened the boy's armor until he was putty. Kenny put his hands in his pockets and cracked a half smile, nodding his head in a bid of truce. Nash felt a flare of annoyance. Felix was on the same page, arms folded and eyes slit with contempt. They were both thinking this Kenny kid was going to have to be the babysat bitch in the bunch.

"Sorry for yelling at you," Kenny said. "I didn't mean to call you a cunt."

Ginger smiled. "Forget about it. It's nothing."

"You sure?"

"I think you can be forgiven under the circumstances—"

Nash's voice could have bit through concrete. "Jesus, when you two little bitches finish finger-banging each other, do you think we can figure out what we're gonna do about this predicament of ours?"

Ginger's face darkened and she spat venomously in his direction, murmuring a string of obscenities. A slap across his face would have satisfied her, but she restrained herself. Instead, she turned to Kenny and thumbed over her shoulder.

"I should probably tell you now, when God created righteous cunts, he made the mold out of Nash over there."

Nash snorted. "You got some fucking nerve, woman—"

A moaning sound came from the sand. The Hispanic girl was starting to come to. Disoriented and mumbling, she lifted her head. When her eyes fixed on the others she instantly rolled away and cowered.

"It's okay, honey," Ginger said. "We don't bite."

The girl didn't answer. Judging by the confusion on her face, Nash wasn't sure she was capable of giving a reply.

"What's your name?" he asked.

The girl swallowed hard, never taking her eyes off them. She was petite, but not fragile. Her dark hair and skin could have been sensuous, if both didn't look so horribly neglected. Felix's rumbling voice visibly rattled her when he spoke.

"Answer the man. What's your *name*?"

Nash frowned. "I don't think she speaks English."

"Oh, she speaks it, alright," Felix said, looking the girl in the eye. "Too many cons have tried to pull the *no Eengleesh* card on me in my time."

Each of them threw a sharp glance her way. The girl swallowed again, but this time answered with a thick Spanish accent.

"Maria is my name."

She drew her knees up under her chin, wrapping her arms around her shins. The eyes that looked around were those of a terrified animal. Kenny sat on the fringe of the grass, scratching at his chest and offering her a weak smile that did nothing to set her at ease. Felix mulled over the scene, looking back toward the foot-print trail with a compulsion that suggested a freshly stuffed candy nose.

Six

Felix Fenton's candy nose burned so bad he thought he might yell. Every vein in his right nostril was aflame. Nasal drip was like acid. The coke he'd bought was of the harshest variety and his sinuses were paying for it. What the hell was it cut with? Salt? Carpet deodorizer? If Felix's sense of smell wasn't so wrecked already he might have sniffed a clue. Blow was always cut with something worthless, that much was true. You couldn't avoid it these days. Pollutants bought from dollar stores caused purity to plummet everywhere. Felix preferred something like powdered baby laxative in his order when he was getting shortchanged. A few extra visits to the crapper he could deal with. This shit, though, jammed up his nose, was all kinds of wrong.

Forty bucks well misspent, but beggars couldn't be choosers.

Don't you dare blow your nose, he thought. *Don't waste a goddamn milligram now. The pain will pass. Wait it out.*

His eyes watered before glazing. There it was—the kick, the payoff that he worried might not come. Felix shuddered, teeth grinding, gums flexing, tongue pressed to the roof of his mouth.

"Fuck yeah."

He rubbed his nose, trying to derail the unreachable itch forming halfway to the back of his throat. The kick was surprisingly decent, but not nearly enough. Felix had to have another. The stairwell of his run-down apartment building was not the wisest spot to indulge. Even so, he crammed himself into a dusty corner, unable to wait another minute. Coke was the appetizer, the link in the chain that connected him to his true anchor, something to tie him over until he got settled in his apartment where he could cook.

"Double down," he muttered and pulled a tiny vial from his jacket pocket.

He tapped another bump into the concave of his long pinky fingernail and pressed it to his nostril. With a piggish snort he vacuumed it into his head. There was pain again, though not as severe as before. The kick was less too, but piggybacked the previous one nicely. It gave

Felix's exhausted legs the energy to bound two steps at a time up the three flights to his floor.

At his landing he considered a third bump. These weren't proper rails he was snorting, mere sprinklings at best. He looked at the vial again, half full with cheap cocaine, and swallowed the bitter chemical that leaked into his throat from his sinuses. The coke called his name again and again. Felix's better half, now shrunk to less than an eighth, chastised him for listening.

You can't wait thirty seconds until you're in the privacy of your own damn home? What the fuck's wrong with you, nigga? Get a grip.

Felix ran that squeaky angel off his shoulder nine times out of ten these days, but he let it cruise this time. Privacy was something he was becoming less mindful of and might pay the price for if he didn't take care. Cops were always looking for an easy bust and Felix, black and male and addicted, was enough of a target already. The vial found its way back inside his pocket.

". . . I'll keep you updated, sir."

An unknown voice up ahead. Felix rounded the corner into his hallway and stopped. Six doors down, shuffling away from his apartment door, was a mystery man. White and suspicious, that was all Felix took into account. He was slipping something into his back pocket as he tried to leave the scene. Felix had no doubt the guy had just been fucking with his front door.

"Hey!"

Felix quickened his step as he approached. The man looked over his shoulder and their eyes met. Felix tried on his mad dog glare, the one he used around the neighborhood regularly to warn others to give him a wide berth. It didn't create an ounce of concern in the man's reciprocating gaze. Felix got within three feet of him and reached out to grab a shoulder.

"Hey, what the fuck do you think—"

Felix had been a boxer at one point in his life, back when it had been important for a sample cup of his piss to come up clean. He saw the right hook coming, despite the uncanny speed of the delivery. Felix weaved, feeling knuckles graze his neck. He countered with a poorly timed uppercut that connected with the man's sternum instead of his chin. The man grunted, but was otherwise unfazed. Felix tried for a headlock.

"Asshole, you just signed your own—"

In a flash the tables were turned. Arms got inside Felix's guard, wrists slipped past his face, easily outmaneuvering his attempt to defend. Before he knew it Felix found himself in a clinch and at the man's mercy.

Death warrant.

He'd underestimated his opponent, a critical mistake. One sentence filled the ticker tape of his thoughts, still transmitting as the first instance of pain came.

This is how it ends.

The man's forearms crushed Felix's head like a vise, compressing his cheekbones, squashing his ears to his head, burning them with friction as he tried to pull free. When the knee came up, Felix wasn't ready. It was like something he'd seen in an underground Muay Thai fight once. The man's knee bore into his gut with such upward force that Felix felt his heels lift off the ground. Seconds later another knee planted in the same spot and the vise grip released. Felix dropped like a puppet with strings slashed, the wind knocked out of him. His breath would not return.

Dude is pro, Felix thought. *That wasn't luck.*

On his knees and doubled over, forehead a foot from the floorboards, Felix knew the misjudgment would cost him. His lungs demanded oxygen, though intake was impossible. He anticipated only two or three seconds before a heel or fist came down on the back of his head, or, worse, a bullet. He could visualize the police report: *murdered execution style.* Felix braced for the sound of a hammer being cocked. Instead he heard a low Texas drawl, the smile behind it as unmistakable as the pained breath in it.

"It's your lucky day, boy. Any other and I'd have finished you for that."

A vicious kick to the ribs flipped Felix on his back. Breathless, he lay there, staring at the discolored, water-damaged stucco of the ceiling, waiting for hands to rifle his pockets and make off with his wallet and contraband. The robbery never came. His attacker was already on his way out, boots clomping back the way Felix had come. One last remark came from down the hall.

"You best count your blessings while you can, man."

Felix dared not move, wheezing, coaxing his lungs to expand enough for a full breath. With strength returning he propped himself against the wall in a sitting position and fought the urge to vomit. He took a tiny baggie out of the inside pocket of his jacket and carefully checked it over, making sure it wasn't damaged in the fight. This was his other purchase, his one true master: that which had made a modern-day slave out of him. The fine white powder inside didn't look much different from what was in the vial, but the two were incomparable to Felix. The heroin held his eyes and gnawed at his brain stem. He thought of freshly fallen snow, a delightful worm wiggling through white drifts. His voice was pained, wispy, when he finally spoke to the empty hallway.

"Hell, you're the most beautiful thing I've ever seen."

Seven

NOW.

"**W**ho knew hell could look so beautiful?" Felix said, eyes skating over the turquoise water, fingers finding their way inside his open shirt to caress the two-day-old bruise on his stomach that was camouflaged from the others by his dark skin.

"We're in hell?" Kenny asked.

"Got a feeling we will be soon enough."

"Fuck, I'm already there," Ginger grumbled and nodded toward Nash. "Who put this clown in charge?"

Nash ignored her. Someone had to handle the situation and none of them seemed willing to step up to the plate. He paced back and forth, arms crossed, voice authoritative.

"Okay," Nash began. "First of all, does anyone remember how they got here?"

They all shook their heads except Ginger. She stood motionless, face pinched, bitterly pissed at him for taking the helm.

"Okay, does anyone know where the hell we *are*?"

Shrugs and silence. After some consideration Felix spoke.

"I'm guessing somewhere in the Florida Keys?"

Nash rolled his eyes. That was a no-brainer. Judging by their surroundings there was little doubt they could be anywhere else.

"No shit, Sherlock. I was hoping for something a little more specific."

Felix flipped him the bird. "Fine, we're on a deserted island in the Florida Keys."

"What do we all have in common?" Nash asked.

Kenny gave a shaky laugh. "Shit, we all got fucking roofied, man."

"Is it safe to assume we're all from Miami?"

Everyone nodded.

"What parts?"

Hesitation from the others as Nash looked from person to person, hoping they might say something first. Lips were sealed, none of them willing. Nash gave in and took a deep breath to get the ball rolling.

"Opa-locka, north near the I-95. I'm in a Wash Box."

They all knew it, the code name for those on the level. There were plenty of bad places to hole up in

Miami, but the Washington Blocks ranked with the worst. They didn't just scrape the bottom of the barrel; they punched a hole through it to an even shadier depth. There was a delay before the rest of them volunteered any information.

"I'm in Overtown," Kenny said eventually. "Wrong side of the tracks, I guess you could say."

"Coconut Grove," said Ginger. "The bad corner."

Nash snickered. "Jeez, which one?"

"The worst one."

"And you?" Nash asked, turning to Felix.

"Liberty City, Seventy-ninth Street, y'all can guess which intersection."

"The one you don't hang out on after sunset?"

"The very same."

Nash turned to Maria. "What about you?"

All eyes were on the woman who spoke little. She wanted no part of the conversation, trying to appear disinterested in them and the talk they were having. Her eyes betrayed her, though, silently informing the others that she was afraid to answer. They stared her down until she capitulated.

"I . . . move around."

"Maria of no fixed address, eh?" Felix said. "Don't sweat it, honey. I've been there too, more than once."

The demographic they shared was clear. Every one of them dangled from the bottom rung of Miami's social ladder, living in the worst neighborhoods with the poorest folk. More destitute urban locations of Western civilization on the East Coast would be hard to find.

"What else we got in common?" Ginger asked.

"I dunno," Kenny said. "It ain't age, sex, or race. I mean, we got man, woman, black, white, young, old—"

Kenny cut himself off and cast a nervous glance at Felix, who sneered before holding up a fist and extending a middle finger at the boy.

"Who the fuck you calling old?"

Nash didn't miss a beat. "Oh, come on. You get a senior's discount with all that gray hair, dude?"

"Premature . . . it comes with the territory."

Nash raised an eyebrow. "And what territory is that?"

Felix didn't reply. Nash looked the man over, then the others, then himself, looking for similarities, wondering what else they shared. He scratched at his sweaty throat, tiny sickly spiders crawling under his skin that needed to be squashed.

"Have any of us ever seen each other before today?"

"Nope," Ginger said, cocking her head as she looked at Nash. "But you're starting to seem a little familiar. What do you do?"

"A bit of this, a bit of that."

"Yeah, don't we all. C'mon, what's your thing?"

"I'm a musician."

"Wait?" Ginger peered at him. "Are you in a band or something?"

"Yeah, mostly play guitar in this outfit called Fuel Injector."

It took a moment before Ginger's eyebrows rose. Then she jabbed a finger at him, a snide bark of laughter punctuating each stab in the air.

"You're in *Fuel Injector*? You play at the Barracuda Room sometimes, right? That band that's always advertising ladies free 'cause you can't get any chicks to show up to your gigs?"

"Bitch, you don't know what you're talking about."

Ginger smirked. She knew exactly what she was talking about.

"I knew I'd seen your washed-up ass on a poster or something somewhere. Man, you look worse than your lame-ass photo."

Nash shrugged off her comment. "Okay, there's something we have in common. We've both been to the Barracuda Room. Felix? You ever been to that joint? It's in Coconut Grove."

"Nah, I stay out of C.G. Made some enemies there a couple years back."

"Kenny? How about you?"

"Nope. Never."

Nash turned to Maria, but she only shook her head and averted her eyes.

Ginger snapped her fingers. "Speaking of enemies, do you guys have any?"

"No one I'd call an enemy per se," Nash said. "There's a seriously pissed-off bass player I shit-canned from the band a few months ago, but that's about it."

Kenny sighed. "My parents hate my guts. Can't think of anyone else who has a problem with me. What about you, Ginger?"

"I run out on a lot of joints without paying my tab," she replied. "Which makes me public enemy number one with local bartenders and waitresses."

Ginger scratched her elbow and for the first time Nash saw, really saw, the track marks on the insides of her forearms, scabby ones dotted with the fresh, their numbers alarming. He looked closer at everyone, discovering similar scarring. The harrowed looks on their faces, the bags under their eyes, the feverish, incessant scratching. All were signs. Nash paused before asking his next question, the precursor of silence making it pop from his lips when he finally spoke.

"You're all junkies, aren't you?"

The question caught Felix, Maria, and Kenny off guard, but not Ginger. She'd already pieced it together. She looked him straight in the eye and an understanding passed between them, two diseased peas sharing a putrid pod.

"Not as dumb as you look," she said.

Uncomfortable silence from the rest, telling Nash everything he needed to know. He scratched another burgeoning itch on his neck to show that he too was a member of their exclusive club. They began to peer at one another for the telltale signs of a bad heroin habit. Only Kenny had less overt signifiers of drug abuse, but he was the youngest. Ginger's fingers crept over the veins in her arms, touching the remnants of every puncture that pockmarked her skin.

"Smack made me its bitch years ago."

The others nodded in perfect unison: addict marionettes strung together. Nash leaned over and inspected Ginger's arms as close as he dared. She allowed him, but only so she could return the favor. It was close, but Nash's looked a mite worse.

"Made all of us its bitch," said Nash. "That's what it does best."

Everyone avoided eye contact, trying to hide their scars and scabs, fiddling with their clothes and hair, pretending to be suddenly interested in their surroundings. The tension in the air implied that no one wanted to continue the conversation. Kenny was the only exception. He raised a hand and waved it until everyone was looking at him.

"So . . . uh, what kind of price do you guys get for your shit?"

Eight

TWO DAYS AGO.

"**H**ow much did that cost you?" Kenny asked.

"No different from anywhere else," Merle replied.

Kenny Colbert shifted his weight uneasily in the leather armchair. He was getting antsy. Looking at the tar turning in Merle's fingers made him twitch with delight.

Matty, on the other hand, sat completely still. His voice was soft, as if raising it might disrupt preparations. "Except this stuff ain't like that weak-ass shit *you* keep buying."

Kenny was defensive. "My shit ain't bad."

Matty and Merle exchanged a smirk on the sofa. Kenny leaned forward in his seat, gawking at them for validation.

"C'mon, my shit ain't *too* bad. . . ."

"Your shit ain't too good either, kid," said Merle. "We gotta expand your palette."

"And you need to learn to take your medicine properly," Matty added, nodding to a syringe lying at the end of the coffee table. "Like a grown-up."

"I told you needles freak me out," Kenny whined. "I ain't sticking myself."

Matty groaned. "Oh, don't be such a pussy. You don't get your money's worth freebasing. You gotta inject for best effect."

"I *don't* like needles, Matty."

"Love this kid," laughed Merle. "No matter what, he sticks to his guns."

Merle reached over and gave Kenny's neck a squeeze, fingers lingering longer than appropriate. Kenny shrugged the grip off and leaned away. He hated being a third wheel to Matty and Merle, or M&M, as they were called. As far as Kenny was concerned, Matty was the only piece of candy between them. His beige skin and curly brown hair, complemented by his almond eyes, were almost too sweet. Merle was bland in comparison. He was much older, gaining weight and graying around the edges, but always had money to blow. Being equal amounts dealer, thief, and pimp, Merle was bringing in a lot of disposable income. His little whore Matty generated a good portion of it too. Being too old to hook himself anymore, Merle had a kind of father-figure complex going on with his escort-in-training, although it didn't stop him burying his dick in Matty when Kenny wasn't around.

And it didn't stop the older man from trying it on with Matty's friends every now and then.

"How much longer?" Kenny asked. "I'm fucking jonesing here."

Kenny looked at the time displayed on a large and completely out of place antique grandfather clock standing next to the fifty-inch flat-screen TV on the opposite wall, both taken in trade. He watched the second hand tick, faster than it should, though time itself was dragging. Kenny needed his hit hours ago.

"Be patient," Matty said. "You want it done right, not done fast."

Merle's cell phone chirped and he retrieved it from his pocket. He was smiling when he looked at the call display. The smile fell when he recognized the number. Creases appeared on his brow. He rose from the couch with a grunt.

"Take over, Matty," he ordered. "I have to take this call."

"Jesus, Merle. C'mon, we're right in the middle of fixing our—"

"You think I don't know that?" Merle spat. "Some things are a little more important than your goddamn tar."

Kenny didn't like the tone of Merle's voice. This was pimp-Merle, the *don't you dare fuck with me* part that revealed itself on occasion. Matty should have folded, but he decided to be a little bitch instead.

"Like *what*, Merle? What's more important than this? Please tell me, because I really, really want to know."

Kenny was sure Matty would receive a slap for his insolence, and he might have, had the incessant ringing of Merle's incoming call not forced the older man to leave the room for some privacy.

"Take care of Kenny," Merle said over his shoulder as he headed for the bedroom. "And prep my dose. I'll be back in ten minutes."

Merle slammed the bedroom door behind him, making Kenny flinch. Matty didn't even bat an eye, taking over the preparations with an unimpressed shake of his head.

"What was that about?" Kenny asked.

Matty shrugged. "Who cares?"

"Don't you?"

Matty rolled his eyes. He wasn't interested in anything his pimp-daddy was talking about. His only interest was the heroin laid out before them. Kenny's curiosity, however, was aroused.

"Is he talking business?" Kenny asked.

"He's always talking business," Matty said. "He doesn't talk anything else."

"What's he got going on these days?"

Matty turned an impatient grin on him. "Hey, you wanna get high or you wanna keep flapping your lips?"

Kenny realized then just how much Matty didn't

want to talk about Merle or Merle's business, probably because it involved his own fine naked form in all kinds of compromising positions.

"High," Kenny said, and he turned his attention back to the junk.

"Wait here a second," Matty whispered.

He tiptoed to the kitchen and rummaged around in some drawers, returning a minute later with a secretive smile on his face and something in his hand.

"I've got a present for you."

"You do?"

"Uh-huh, but don't tell Merle, okay?"

"I won't. Cross my heart."

Matty held out his hand, a small packet of white powder in his palm. "Forget that tar, I'm treating you to something better. Merle picks up from this particular connection once in a while. It's not too often, only when the supplier comes into town, which is a pity because this shit is incredible. It comes from Afghanistan, straight from the source. That's where they grow the best poppies on the planet."

"Yeah?" Kenny grinned. "Awesome."

"Oh, you don't know the half of it, sweetheart. Quality control is in short supply these days, but this here is triple-A rated. You ready for your medicine?"

"Yeah, just let me take a leak first."

Kenny rose and made his way to the bathroom. If the

stuff was as good as Matty was saying, he worried about wetting himself. Once, while tripping, Kenny's bladder had relaxed involuntarily under the influence of premium quality. He passed the closed bedroom door where Merle was taking his phone call and heard a muffled voice speaking rapidly with stress. Curious, Kenny strained to hear the conversation, figuring Merle was talking to a prospective client about Matty and his services.

". . . Look, I know what type of guy you need. I'm just saying he's not a bad boy. . . . Yeah, I understand, you don't need to remind me of that. . . . Look, a deal's a deal. Have I ever not come through before? He's what you want . . . he fits your *profile* . . . yes . . . yes . . . I'll have him gift-wrapped for you in less than twenty-four hours. . . ."

Kenny leaned away from the door, no longer comfortable with wanting to hear the sordid details of what sexual favors Matty was capable of providing for what prices. His friend never spoke much about what he did to earn his keep and Kenny felt suddenly guilty for eavesdropping. His own parents, people of wealth and influence, had argued regularly in the privacy of their bedroom when he was a child. Cupping a curious ear to their closed door had been one of his biggest regrets, an action that led him to discover the extent of the hatred his father had for his "faggot son." His mother wasn't much better, convinced that Kenny's homosexuality was a phase, and that with the help of prayer and patience, God would straighten him out. Wishful thinking, Kenny knew even back then. At sixteen he was kicked out of the house after being caught in the basement with his hand down the pants of an older boy. In less than twenty-four hours he was on the street with nothing but the suitcase his mother had packed and his father's final words still ringing in his ears.

You made your choice to be an affront to God, son. Your mother and I don't ever want to see you again.

Kenny took his piss and returned to the living room, perturbed by memories, not wanting them in his head anymore. The junk would help. He wished he had the balls to cross the line to injection, but freebasing was his m.o. After all, Kenny sucked like a vacuum cleaner. Numerous men could testify to that.

"Here's the prom queen." Matty chuckled. "Just in time."

Kenny plopped down in the armchair. Matty had his hit prepped, lighter already cooking the underside of an aluminum foil square. Kenny's eyes strayed to the syringe nearby. Matty noticed.

"Thinking about a change in tactics?"

"I'm thinking about it."

"Why now?"

"I want the whole nine yards. I want to chase away

my demons and not have them come knocking for a while."

Matty smiled. "Smoking or shooting, this shit will do that regardless. I promise."

"I hate this stupid hang-up I have with needles. . . ."

"Next time, Kenny," Matty cooed. "We'll hook it up for you next time."

"Fucking things scare me. They always have."

Matty caressed Kenny's hand. "Look, I'll shoot you up myself when you're ready. You'll barely even feel the pinch when that junk hits your bloodstream, okay? But for now just stick with what works for you."

Kenny looked at the syringe again. "What's it like, shooting that stuff?"

Matty grinned. "It's like . . . having this wonderful wiggly worm inside your head."

He held out the hit. Kenny leaned forward with his pipe and inhaled the fumes rising from the foil until his relaxing muscles caused him to fall back into the cushions. He closed his eyes, diving headfirst into the drug's euphoria, the plunge peeling away his worries and stretching time over the ticking of the grandfather clock. Faintly, in the center of his head, he was sure he could sense that worm Matty was talking about, wiggling, dancing, making love to his gray matter. Kenny trilled with delight.

"Best shit ever."

Nine

"**G**ood shit is harder than ever to get," Kenny said. "But I still score some prime now and then."

"Yeah, I heard Overtown rolls out some good grade," said Felix. "In Liberty City you're lucky if you don't get jacked with a score of baking soda. I've blown B.S. up my arm more than a few times."

"Buying off a corner is a fucking fool's game," Ginger said. "You got to get in with a dealer you can trust."

Felix thrust his hips forward. "Or let a dealer get in you, right?"

Ginger thought of Curtis. "Bite me."

Felix laughed. "Hell no, honey, you'd bite back."

A wry smile curled the corners of Ginger's mouth. Felix warmed to it.

"Who am I to judge anyway?" he continued. "You wouldn't believe the shit I done for tar in my day."

"Fuck, can we stop talking about dope for a minute?" Nash said, clutching his pained stomach. "You guys are making me hungry."

"Shit, man, what else is there to do?" Felix said, looking around at the sea and sand. "You wanna go for a dip? Work on your tan?"

"I want to get some answers."

"And how do you plan to do that?"

"Well, it appears there's someone else on this island we ain't met yet." Nash stood carefully, so as not to strain the ache in his gut. He pointed toward the footprints leading from the beach to the grass and trees. "I say we follow the trail."

Felix shrugged. No one seemed to have a better suggestion. Nash took the lead, the others falling in behind. Only Ginger held back, reluctant to be led by the likes of a man she was at odds with. Kenny glanced back repeatedly, his worried eyes insistent that she follow.

"C'mon, Ginger."

She ran to catch up, knowing the boy wouldn't fare well without her. They hiked single file through the brush, tramping down tall grass and swatting aside branches, following the trail as best they could. Once they passed the tree line they were engulfed by leaves and bark. Hot, muggy air stuck to their skin inside the thicket. Insects buzzed in the vegetation and scuttled out of their way. Within minutes they'd transgressed the small forest center to the opposite side of what was indeed an island, no more than several hundred yards in width. Another beach came into view, looking identical to the one they had just come from, except for the solitary human being sitting on the sand a hundred yards up the shoreline.

Nash turned to Felix. "How about we go introduce ourselves to Robinson fucking Crusoe over there?"

Felix gave Nash a sly smile. "Try calling me your man Friday at some point, see what happens."

Felix chuckled at Nash's wide-eyed look of surprise and took the lead, making his way toward the new player on the beach. The stranger did not appear to notice. As they neared they saw he was seated next to a metal trunk, lid flipped open. Felix called out, but the man didn't react. He only watched from the corner of his eye. Felix broke into a jog, arriving on the man's scene ahead of the others.

"Who you?" Felix said with a jab of his chin.

The mulatto's eyes were dull, his smirk even more so. No doubt he was one of their kind, track marks and all. He looked the oldest and most abused out of everyone. Erratic nappy hair, clothes in shit state, scratches and scars peppering every exposed piece of beige skin. In the center of his gray, nicotine-stained beard was a trace of a smile that simply said *I am incapable of giving a shit about anything anymore*. Ginger and Kenny both took a curious step toward the open trunk, but the man stopped them with a glance. Felix stepped closer to the man so as to tower over him.

"Hey, I asked you a question."

No answer. With a grunt Felix balled his hands into fists. Nash jumped in, knowing that Felix was aching for an excuse to beat on someone.

"Nash, Felix, Ginger, Kenny, Maria, that's us," Nash said, waving a hand toward each person to match him or her with a name. "C'mon, let's start off on the right foot. What's your name, pal?"

"Tallahassee Jones," replied the man lazily. "Call me Tal, if you must."

Felix sucked air through his teeth, but his hands relaxed. Nash breathed a sigh of relief. He wanted no violence today, black on black or otherwise.

"Tal it is," said Nash. "You have any idea what's going on? Or are you as much in the dark as we are?"

"I got a bit of light to shed," he replied. "It ain't much, though."

Tal dipped his lined forehead toward the open trunk beside him. Maria hung back, afraid, but the other four stationed themselves at the corners and looked inside. Neatly placed in the confines were six sandwiches

72

wrapped in plastic, an armful of apples, a box of energy bars, and a dozen bottles of water.

"What's this, a frigging *picnic*?" Ginger seethed.

The others were speechless. Wedged between the bottles and the side of the trunk was a plain white envelope torn open at one end.

"Okay, can someone please explain this to me?" Kenny whined. "Like, right fucking now?"

No one said anything. Kenny looked back and forth between Nash and Felix, wanting someone to say something that made a shred of sense. Every passing second of silence added another dent in his worried expression. Maria inched her way to the box and leaned in for a look, braced as if she expected something to spring out and attack her. Felix reached inside and picked up one of the sandwiches. He turned it over in his hands, wondering if it might be poisoned.

"Ham and cheese, anyone?" he said.

"You first," Ginger said. "Age before beauty."

Felix snorted. "No one beautiful around here as far as I can tell."

"Read what's in the envelope," Tal advised.

Ginger reached for the envelope, but Nash beat her to it. He slid the folded letter out, a paragraph of black type on white unfolding before his eyes. The others held their breath. Nash read the message aloud, slowly, carefully.

"Dear civilians,

"Please know that no one will be coming to your aid. Much effort has been made to ensure this. Enjoy what has been provided, but also know that it is all the sustenance you shall receive here. Food and water will only get you so far, as there is something else you desire, and will continue to more and more as time passes. If you want your next hit, you will have to earn it. Your target is the island across the channel to the north, where another box of supplies awaits. This one also contains an allotment of the purest, highest-quality heroin you will ever experience, guaranteed. Further instructions are in the next box. Begin whenever you wish."

There was one additional line that Nash failed to mention to the others. He read it silently to himself as he folded the note.

You are being observed at all times.

Dumbstruck silence followed. The letter's contents were too much for everyone to digest at once. Nash held on to the note. No one seemed to want to read it for themselves. Tal eyed Nash with a raised eyebrow, fully aware that the last line had been left out.

"Who the hell left this for us?" squawked Kenny.

"My bet is on *them*," Tal said and stood.

He outstretched his arm and pointed a crooked finger at the sea. Beyond was the target island referred to in the letter, roughly a mile out from where they stood. Anchored in the water between them and the island was a large motor yacht.

"A boat?" asked Maria, eyes alight with hope.

Nash was shocked that none of them except Tal had noticed until now. As soon as Kenny saw it he ran to the edge of the water, arms flailing.

"Hey!" he yelled. "Hey! Over here!"

Ginger and Felix were quick to join in the frantic flagging. Tal chuckled at the furor of the three and turned a wry smile on Nash. Nash didn't like it. It was an extension of Tal's *I can't give a shit anymore* expression that suggested something more sinister.

I think I preferred being in the dark, Nash thought.

He and Maria peered at the stationary boat. The distance didn't allow for much detail, but Nash could make out the dark shapes of two figures standing on the bow of the white vessel. The commotion on the shore was not stirring a reaction from them, yet it was clear they were looking in the right direction. Soon a third figure emerged and joined the other silhouettes. The three stood motionless, observing the six stranded souls on the distant beach.

"C'mon, we're not that far away," Felix said, dread-locks shaking in disbelief.

He waved his arms once more and stopped. Ginger had already quit. The lack of participation from Nash, Maria, and Tal told her all she needed to know. Kenny kept up his antics, unhampered by the others' refusal to continue.

"Are they goddamn *blind*?" shrieked Kenny. "We're right fucking *here*!"

"They can see us," said Nash. "They know we're here, because they're the ones that put us here."

Kenny whirled around, shocked eyes tearing up, baby face twisted into a pulsating pink knot. The look of defeat on all their faces angered and terrified him at once, prompting him to kick at the sand.

"This is *bullshit*."

A breeze ruffled the paper in Nash's hand, attracting the attention of Felix. He signaled for the note and Nash passed it to him. Felix read it over silently. He too failed to make mention of the last line to the others.

"It's from those guys," said Felix. "It has to be. That boat and this letter are one and the same."

"What do they want from us?" asked Maria.

"They want us to make our move."

"Our move?" whined Kenny. "What is it we're supposed to do?"

It was obvious from the letter what they were

supposed to do, but no one spoke, no one wanted to admit as much. Their gazes drifted from the boat to the channel that separated them from the other island. It looked relatively calm, shades of blue darkening with the depths away from shore. Despite its serenity, the idea of traversing it churned their guts. A mile was a hell of a distance to swim, and Christ knew what was lurking in those waters.

"We'd never make it anyway," Felix said finally.

"We might," said Nash.

From the corner of his eye Nash saw Tal scratch his ear like a dog with fleas. In front of him Ginger raked her nails feverishly over the skin on the back of her neck. Another cramp twisted Nash's intestines. Kenny kicked sand in the direction of the next island, showering grains into the water.

"Fuck *that*," spat Kenny. "No frigging way. Not doing it. Never gonna happen."

There was silent agreement. It was suicide. The six of them stood defiantly on the shore and did not move for quite some time. Neither did the three figures on the boat.

"This could go on all damn day," Tal finally said and walked away.

Ten

"**T**his could go on all damn day," Tal muttered.

Slim pickings was an understatement. The ball cap at his feet still didn't have a single bill in it. Tallahassee Jones looked up and down the boardwalk again. There were people about, not as many as he'd hoped, but enough to warrant an evening of musical offerings, in his opinion. The cap suggested otherwise.

"C'mon, people, pay a little and I'll play a lot."

Tal mopped his brow with a bandana. The sun was too hot, despite the lateness of the day. The sky was almost cloudless. Not a single breeze from the ocean. He'd spent the better part of the week strumming his mangy acoustic on the boardwalk and asking folks for spare change in the sweltering heat. Change was all that was being tossed his way, sparse and of the nickel and

79

dime variety. Between songs he swigged from a paper bag containing tall boys of Budweiser. The beer being sucked through his lips was warm and sour, but he didn't care. He got the numbing he needed out of it.

"Christ, folks, throw a dog a bone," he grumbled.

Tal drained his second tall boy of the evening, letting a thimbleful of foamy amber trickle from the corner of his mouth. He let out a loud belch and crushed the can inside the bag, much to the distaste of an old white woman walking her Yorkshire terrier nearby.

"Disgusting," she said.

"Take your bitch elsewhere, bitch," he muttered.

But she was already walking away, pulling her yappy dog along by the neck. The beer buzz chased away his inhibitions and Tal decided to let loose. He tuned his D string, cleared his throat, and broke into a fervent version of Bob Marley's "Waiting in Vain," guitar strumming solid, voice a smoky tenor. He performed with eyes shut, opening them only to thank a passerby when he heard the clink of coins hitting coins in the hat. Whenever Tal played "Waiting in Vain" these days, he didn't think of an elusive love. In fact, a woman was the last thing to come to mind. Now he only equated the lyrics with heroin.

"It's been three years since I'm knockin' on your door . . ."

Three years since heroin completely took over Tal's

life. Before that he'd claimed recreational use for a long time, a baby habit, if such a thing could ever be said of junk. *Recreational* was an almost impossible adjective for the opiate that could never be kept at arm's length, and about as laughable as the term *high-functioning addict*. With heroin you were only delaying the inevitable. Baby habits were quick to turn into belly habits, wringing your guts in an iron grip if you failed to feed them on time.

"Tears in my eyes burn, tears in my eyes burn . . ."

Tal had cried for heroin. He'd begged for it, crawled for it, fought for it, stole for it, and once almost killed for it.

"Sounds awesome, dude," said a kid passing by on a skateboard.

Tal nodded appreciatively, but the kid donated nothing. Busking outside the marina was usually lucrative, more profitable than mere panhandling. People with the money and the means liked to see the less fortunate work for a handout. They wanted entertainment for their dollar, whether it be singing on a sidewalk or dancing on a bed of hot coals. Those who moored their boats at the marina all had serious dough. Some of them recognized Tal and tossed him a little extra, though it still made him feel like a minstrel most days. Once in a while some specimens of white wealth would walk by and regard him as such, a sneer on their lips or a chuckle in their throat. Tal had half a mind to bash their heads in with his guitar. Give him enough tall boys in one afternoon and he just might.

Tal looked at the expensive yachts on the water, wishing he had the kind of bank account that paid for them. He took in their names: *Odyssey Two*, *North Star*, *Esmeralda*, *Pelican Briefs*, *The Naughty Nemo*. Some were sailing toward the Florida Keys, toward the place Tal dreamed of escaping on a pricey pleasure craft with a few hot bitches at his disposal and a mountain of coke in the cabin. He knew more about the Keys than the average Joe. His years working as a janitor at the marina had given him the knowledge, back before he got fired for trespassing on people's docked vessels.

"Shit job anyway," Tal mumbled, tuning his E string.

During his employment he'd overheard much at the marina. Scores of Jimmy Buffetts with one too many margaritas down the hatch had given Tal insight into high-class life on the water. Tal took notes, a habit that had eventually led him to board boats in search of things to boost. He knew how much these vessels sold for, how much fuel they consumed, how much their insurance cost, how much they depreciated over time. He knew what parts could be stolen and sold for a pretty penny too. A fish finder could go for hundreds of dollars, marine radar for thousands.

The Keys themselves, though, they were a thing of interest. Over seventeen hundred islands of various shapes and sizes made up the archipelago, a network of dotted land and separating sea covering more than three hundred and fifty square miles. Tal knew just how lost you could get in those parts. Every year a number of boats failed to return to the marina.

Some vanish without a trace, Tal thought.

The Keys could be cruel. Unbearable heat, freak weather, rocks and reef hiding just below the surface primed to puncture hulls. Plenty of ways a person could fuck up their boat trip too: miscalculate fuel, run out of supplies, or simply suck at navigation. If your boat ran into trouble, that was one thing; but if it went down, you were toast. Adrift in a dinghy or floating in a life jacket gave you a snowball's chance in hell of surviving. Even with a radio or phone to call for help, you would be waiting ages for rescue if you didn't have exact coordinates. You'd be the proverbial needle in a haystack, a human speck on a vast canvas of blue. Whether people were searching or not didn't really change how long it might take for someone to come across you out there.

There were far worse places to die in the world, Tal conceded that. The Keys were sensually beautiful, the epitome of paradise. The tropical sun, sand, and sea might make you think you'd died and gone to heaven. But Tal knew the allure was part of the deception. The postcard scenes were silken veils drawn across untrust-worthy faces. The things out there that could cut you, sting you, paralyze you, devour you—too many to remember.

When missing boat owners reappeared they were usually in corpse form. Hurricane season was a death sentence for anyone caught out in the Keys. The lucky ones drowned. The less fortunate died of hunger or thirst. The poorest souls succumbed to the stuff of night-mares. Nature had a habit of mixing beauty with beast. The Keys were no exception. Its beasts were blood-thirsty.

Tal remembered a fishing trip he'd taken long ago with some friends he hadn't seen now in years. There had been warnings from the outset, and cautionary tales told during lunch on an island. Their skipper, reeking of whiskey and cigarettes, made sure everyone under-stood that to be taken in by the Keys' charms was fool-ish, citing the case of his own brash brother who had gone scuba diving one morning and never returned.

Tal couldn't recall the details much, but he did remember the skipper's stories scaring him enough to consider passing on the snorkeling portion of the trip. When he did get in the water he stayed close to the boat, refusing to venture out too far. Through his face mask he saw all he needed to: shallows fanning out and sud-denly dropping down into rock and reef where small fish swam in schools and crustaceans scuttled over coral sharp enough to flay flesh from bone.

It was what he didn't see that would have convinced him to stay out of the water for good. Farther out, larger creatures swam in the cooler, darker, deeper waters where sunlight was gradually eaten away until the gloom was almost liquid night. Far fewer species ventured down into the blind cold. Those that did rarely returned. From time to time the last straining rays of sunlight would be broken by large gliding bodies that were known to patrol the depths—creatures that also ventured to the surface.

You'll never catch me diving down there, Tal thought, looking out at the expanse of ocean beyond the marina.

He began strumming his guitar again, determined to earn a score's worth of pity from passersby. The sun was sinking to the horizon. The lampposts along the boardwalk buzzed, gathering enough charge to flicker weak light. He broke into his third tall can and looked up and down the walk to see if any cops were around. Hardly anyone about at all, so he decided on another Marley number, a down-tempo version of "I Shot the Sheriff." Tal closed his eyes and played.

"Every time I plant a seed, he said kill it before it grow. . . ."

Tal strummed and sang with everything he had. When the last chord rang out he opened his eyes. There hadn't been one single clink in the hat during the song, but some generous soul had recognized his talent and dropped a silent ten-dollar bill. Tal looked around for who that might have been. There was nobody about, save a couple of joggers. Only a sliver of sun showed above the horizon. A thirst inside Tal made itself known, right on cue. Beer wouldn't suffice anymore. There was a habit to feed and tar to score. Tal considered calling it early and heading back to his hood. He looked down at the hat. Almost enough cash inside for one decent fix.

"Maybe I can swing a discount."

Tal looked at his fingers, blistered and raw from all the playing he'd done over the previous days. Enough was enough. He packed up his guitar and pocketed the change. On the way home he'd visit his new dealer, a pusher in the neighborhood known only as Al Catraz. What he'd scored from Catraz the other day was powdered perfection. He needed more of it.

People came and went from the marina all the time and at all hours. Tal thought nothing of the approaching footsteps behind him just before capable arms grabbed and restrained him. The pinch of a needle in his neck swirled and slowed Tal's world. Everything went black by the time he buckled and dropped.

Eleven

NOW.

Tal fell to the sand, hands clutching his upset stomach. The others nearby knew how he felt, for their own guts roiled and burned in their bellies. Felix picked sand out of his belly button and got Nash's attention with a grunt.

"We're civilians to them," he said.

Nash stopped biting his fingernails long enough to ask, "Pardon?"

"They referred to us as civilians in the note," Felix said. "Not citizens, not prisoners, not hostages."

"So?"

"So, why point us out like that? Who calls people civilians?"

Nash thought it over. "Government, I guess."

Felix shook his head. "Military."

"Military?"

"Yeah, or something like it. You're looking at people with power and capability and reach who see people like us as something less, something weaker."

"What are you getting at?" asked Ginger.

Felix looked to the yacht. "I'm not sure yet."

"Then do us all a favor and stop talking," Tal grumbled.

Felix didn't think he'd heard right. He looked at the half-caste sweating on the sand, knees drawn to his chest, facial muscles flexed in a portrait of pain.

"Huh?"

Tal didn't look at him. The agony burning at his core scrunched him up like a paper ball. With eyes squeezed shut and a locked jaw he spoke even quieter than before.

"Quit talking already."

Felix's chuckle was frigid. "What you say to me, boy?"

Tal's scream sent them all reeling. *"I said shut the fuck up, nigger!"*

It took Felix a second to recover from Tal's outburst. Then he was on his feet, fists up, ready to throw down.

"Okay, asshole, round one, let's go."

"Felix!" Nash yelled. "It's not him, it's the dope."

Felix didn't care. Tal didn't rise to the challenge, but Felix struck him anyway, landing an awkward downward punch to the forehead as he fell on the man. Stunned, Tal wrapped his limbs around Felix's body and locked him up. They rolled on the beach, a writhing tangle of black and brown. Felix roared, trying to find purchase for another strike.

"Think you can talk to me like that, you filthy half-breed?"

Tal's arm slipped and Felix managed another swing, but missed his mark, planting a fist into the sand beside Tal's head.

"Nigger?" Felix was saying. "*Nigger?* I'll show you—"

Felix saw the head butt coming, turning his face away just as Tal's forehead crashed into his cheek and blossomed heat there. It probably hurt Tal more, but it still stung Felix like a bitch, spiking his anger up to rage.

"Oh, you're dead for real now, man!"

Nash and Ginger reached around Felix and grabbed an arm each, using all their strength to pull him off Tal and drag him back. Kenny and Maria tried to assist, but managed only to get in the way.

"Jesus, Felix!" Ginger yelled. "Fucking stop!"

Nash backed her. "Quit fighting already."

Felix fought off their grip and they dropped him on his back. He was quick to get to his feet, poised for another fight. Although his expression said he'd take them all on if he had to, he refrained from doing so.

"Touch me again and you'll be the ones on the

receiving end of this," Felix warned, raising a fist. "Mark my words."

Nash and Ginger stepped back, hands raised, not wanting a fight. Tal lay on the sand, breathing hard, staring at the sky with watery, bloodshot eyes. He didn't care if Felix came back for another round. He figured the bruiser couldn't hurt him any more than what was wringing and stabbing his insides.

"The guy is going through withdrawal, dude!" Nash yelled at Felix. "Look at him. He's in agony. He don't mean no harm. He barely knows what he's saying or doing."

Felix looked into Tal's absentee eyes, saw the fever on his face, the sweat on his body, the reddening patches where scratching had raked his skin raw. All of it told him that Tal had already arrived in hell's lobby and would be checking in soon enough. Everyone would be accommodated sooner or later, no exceptions, no escape. The reality of it was starting to erode everyone's composure.

"Had enough?" Felix asked. "Or do you want some more of the same?"

No response. Tal's obliviousness to the threat of attack stopped Felix from launching one. There was an understanding. He'd been in Tal's shoes before, desperate for dope and unable to get fixed. Felix didn't feel pity, but he was struck with anxiety: worry over his own worsening condition that was simply Tal's on a time delay. Ginger stepped forward and laid a hand on Felix's shoulder, supporting his fears.

"Tal's got a head start on the rest of us. I'd say he's in deeper by a day or so."

"Whatever," Felix said. "That still doesn't give him the right to—"

"No, it doesn't, you're right, Felix. All I'm saying is that the withdrawal is a reason, not an excuse, for his bullshit. Let's see how mild mannered you are in twelve to twenty-four hours."

Nash grabbed a bottle of water from the box and knelt beside Tal, extending it to the man's unmoving hand. Tal didn't grab for it.

"Tal, you okay?"

Tal's throat bucked before answering. "Oh, yeah, I'm solid gold. Twenty-four fucking carats, man."

Ginger shored up beside Nash, kneeling so she could lay the back of her hand on the hot skin of Tal's forehead. She felt the lump delivered by Felix's blow.

"How bad you got it, man?"

"You been through it before, honey?" Tal asked, a tear escaping the corner of his eye and rolling to his earlobe. "Gone cold turkey?"

"I've tried to kick the habit a few times, yeah."

"And how'd that make you feel?"

Ginger swallowed hard. "Like a sack of smashed ass-holes."

Tal gave a weak grin. "That's putting it mildly. I'd wager I'm worse off than any of you have ever been before. I ain't got a bad habit. The bad habit's got me. Know what I mean?"

She did. Tal rolled onto his side, away from Ginger. It pained him to do so, but he didn't want the woman to see him cry.

"What do you want us to do?" Kenny asked.

"I want you to go away," Tal moaned and closed his eyes.

It wasn't a request. They did as asked, backing away from Tal as if he were the carrier of an infectious disease.

"And stay away," he added.

The group said no more to each other, breaking off and heading in separate directions. Worsening withdrawal was heightening their irritability, making them sour. Thinking straight was becoming problematic. So was controlling their emotions. Staying sharp required effort now, but they were still wise enough to know that a little distance was a good thing.

Ginger was right. Tal was by far the worst off. The pain became unbearable as he lay on the sand and he was soon forced to stand. He walked the island aimlessly until he found a sizable rock at the far end and perched on it, twisting his back in such a way that it brought relief to his guts. The sight of the small island across the channel fascinated him, its size and distance eating up his attention. Goose bumps stood out on his skin. Itching was incessant on all parts of his body. He talked nonsense to himself and the others were happy to leave him alone.

Ginger and Kenny retreated to the opposite side of the island, where they had first awakened. They took with them their allotment of food, though they had no appetite. Their stomachs ached, producing cold sweat on their skin and low moans in their throats. Girl and boy sat huddled on the sand, feverishly keeping an eye out for any sign of a passing vessel or aircraft.

Nash strolled, patrolling the island's perimeter, lost in his thoughts. Maria took refuge under the shade of a large palm tree, closing her eyes in the vain hope that she might soon wake from her nightmare. Felix seemed to disappear completely, but Nash caught sight of him squatting among the bushes. Nash knew the deal. Diarrhea was the direct result of not taking your junk on time, a reverse of the constant constipation suffered when on the stuff. Vomit played counterpart to this. If Felix hadn't tossed chunks already, he would soon enough.

Nash puked up bile behind a tree where he was sure

no one could see him. Embers burning in his bones flared up and ignited his muscles, white-hot agony causing starbursts in his vision. Cold shivers followed, which seemed to drop a degree with every shudder they produced.

I've never had it so bad in all my life, he thought, wincing as another pang speared his gut.

Despite the varied symptoms between them, the one thing that savaged the six in unison was the hunger. Their cravings had grown exponentially since they had awakened and Nash was well aware of how bad things could get. He'd only attempted a detox once in his life, and that was with the right supplies. He was in for a rough one. They all were.

Nash avoided Tal the first two times he circled the island. On his third pass, he decided to check in. He approached Tal cautiously, watching him sway atop his perch. Before Nash uttered a word, he knew Tal's condition had worsened.

"How are you keeping, buddy?"

A grunt rattled from Tal's throat. Not even a glance was thrown Nash's way. The man stared ahead, lips moving, but making no sound. His knees were drawn up under his chin and he rocked in that unstable way Ginger had when Nash first awoke.

Mental patient, Nash thought. *Victim in shock.*

Tal was almost unrecognizable from the man Nash

had first met on the beach. His face had become more haggard, his eyes feral and bloodshot. His arms were scratched to the point where blood was spotting on the skin from old track marks and spread in freshly raked lines.

"We could make it," Tal suddenly blurted out. "I could . . . yeah . . . fuck, I could make that. S'not that far. Not that far at all."

Nash looked out to where Tal was staring. The next island seemed closer from this vantage point, but he knew it was an illusion. Tal snapped his face toward Nash, eyes wild and popping.

"Not far, not far, not far. Just a little swim, Nash. . . ."

"What?"

"Just a little swim, that's all. Kick, kick, stroke, stroke, and we'd be over there before you know it!"

Tal was serious, his intention backed by a cocksure crazed look, a daredevil with no safety net, oblivious to the dangers. Spittle formed in the corners of his mouth as he leaned forward on his stone throne. A foul fecal smell pricked Nash's nostrils. He suspected the man may have shit his pants and took a step back.

"You could definitely use a dunk in that water, buddy," Nash said. "Smell like you've just rolled out of some homeless guy's asshole."

Tal didn't hear. He glanced back at the channel, grinning like a clown on cocaine, nodding excitedly.

"You and me, N-N-Nash," he gibbered. "Both of us, man. W-we could do it. Swim that shit easy. Just the two of us. More junk if it's just the *two* of us, eh? We get more if it's only me and you, right?"

Nash felt the overwhelming urge to smack the piss out of the stinking, driveling addict. Somehow he thought a beating would make them both feel better. He fought the urge. Nash was well versed with the addicted brain. You couldn't beat sense into, or stupidity out of, a junkie. It would be a waste of time and knuckle skin.

"You're losing it, man," Nash said. "If you think we're swimming to that island you're completely fucked."

Tal shot him a wavering look, his mouth curling into an expectant smile, then dropping into a hopeless gape. His dancing pupils were pinpoints as he mumbled a string of static, unintelligible words.

"Right," Nash said, rolling his eyes. "Point taken."

He turned away, tuning out the maniac's murmurings, bereft of any desire to try to communicate with the increasing half-wit. Tal focused on the water again, hand swaying in front of his face in sync with the movement of the waves. Nash walked only a few paces before swiveling back. All too soon it could easily be him perched on that rock, slowly losing his marbles. He had to at least try. Nash cleared his throat, trying to make his voice as authoritative as possible.

"Come on, Tal. Get down from there and pull your shit together. It's high time we got back to the others."

He may as well have been speaking into a gale-force wind. His words reached no one. Tal was as good as gone, drifting away on his rock, everything meaningless except the next island and the junk on its shore. Nash hitched in breath to repeat, but expelled the air without a word. There was nothing he could do. He flipped Tal the bird instead and turned his back.

"Fine, stay here and rot on your rock."

Walking up the beach, Nash cast another glance toward the water. Among the rolling blue waves and white crests, he caught a flash of gray, gone as quickly as it appeared. Nash waited to see if it would resurface. When it didn't he looked to Tal, wondering if the man had seen it too, but Tal's head was tilted toward the sky, mouth opening and closing like a guppy. Nash trudged back up the beach with a new weight in the pit of his stomach. That which had surfaced in the water preyed on his mind. He wasn't entirely sure, but he thought he'd seen a fin.

When he passed Maria sitting under her tree, his perturbed expression did not go unnoticed. She reached out a stopping hand.

"Hey, what made your face like that?"

Twelve

YESTERDAY.

"What happened to your face?" Maria asked, pointing.

Pablo gave her a slightly annoyed look. Maria had wanted to ask Pablo that question since the first day they'd met. She was finally drunk enough to do it. Each of Pablo's scars called out, inviting Maria's curiosity. The woman slurred her words, further thickening her heavy Cuban accent.

"How did it get like that?"

"How do you mean?" Pablo asked.

"Like all cut up and shit."

She could tell Pablo didn't want to talk about it. He dragged his fingers over the three slim scars that raked his left cheek, and then ran his thumb over the two thick ones near his sideburn. The ugly excrescence that cleaved his forehead he avoided touching altogether. Maria figured the worst memory came with that one.

"Knives made my face like this mostly," he said finally. "But some are from fire."

Pablo picked up the bottle of malt liquor at his feet, turned away, and took a long drink. Maria wanted to ask who had used the knives and fire on the short Mexican, and why, but held her tongue. There were a lot of rumors going around about her companion. Some said he had connections to the cartels. Some said he was a snitch. Everyone knew he was more addict than dealer. In the glow of a single bare bulb that hung above a nearby restaurant back door, Maria saw more marks, small and white, on the nape of his neck. Pablo was the most scarred man she'd ever seen.

"They're from a long time ago," Pablo said. "Another lifetime."

He stood and stretched, inspecting the alleyway he and Maria had chosen for their fix. There was never a time when Pablo didn't seem paranoid, but with all the cuts and burns he'd collected over the years, Maria didn't think it strange.

"A couple of them were accidental," he continued. "But the rest . . ."

Maria held up a hand. "S'okay, you don't have to say no more."

Pablo nodded and took another swig. Maria drank

from her can of cheap beer, crushing the tin inadvertently in her shaky grip. She was jonesing for a hit. Pablo hadn't shown her what he'd scored from around the corner yet and Maria was getting desperate for a glimpse.

"That stuff you got us. It's good shit, no?"

Pablo patted the breast pocket of his checkered shirt. "It don't get any better than this, *chica*."

"Well, what we waiting for?"

Pablo looked around the alley again, unsure. Maria could sense that something wasn't quite right. He scanned the brick walls, scrutinizing shadows, looking for anything that might seem out of place. Both of them had been shaken down by cops in recent days, but luckily neither was holding at the time. If they did get cornered with possession, Maria would give up Pablo in a heartbeat. She had a bad habit of throwing others under the bus to help maintain her own freedoms.

"I don't want anyone intruding on us," Pablo said. "Just wanna make sure we got some privacy."

Maria had a way of dealing with uninvited guests who encroached on her cooking. She would simply hold up a dirty needle and ask them if they wanted HIV. It was an empty threat, as far as she knew, but enough to scare anyone off. Looking at Pablo, Maria didn't know if he was more worried about getting caught with a bubbling spoon or with his pants around his ankles. She wondered which they would do first. The dope was all she wanted. She'd only take Pablo between her legs first if he threatened to hold out on her with the goods.

"S'okay, Pablo," Maria said. "No one will disturb us. Let's get started."

Pablo looked at her, uncertain. Another full sweep of his surroundings drew a shrug out of him and he stood down.

"Fine," he said and began to undo his belt buckle.

Maria hesitated. "You want fuck first?"

"Don't you?"

"I like being high when we do it."

"I don't."

It was an argument she couldn't win. Maria reluctantly removed her pants and sat down on a piece of flattened cardboard, the cleanest she could find in the alley. She didn't take off her panties; those she would pull to one side when Pablo was hard enough. It would take him a little time before he was.

She watched as Pablo exposed his penis and began stroking it. She refused to suck it to get him started. The man's body odor was offensive at the best of times, since he only showered once or twice a week. There was a hint of piss in the air whenever they screwed, sometimes a sweaty old cheese smell too. There was a limit to how low Maria would stoop.

"You doing okay there?"

Pablo's breath came harder, but he didn't answer. His

caressing wasn't getting the desired result. Maria didn't care. Hell, she didn't even like him that much. They only hung out because Pablo was good at scoring smack when she needed it, and he allowed her to pay for her share with sexual favors. Maria never had money, not back when she lived in Cuba, and not since she'd found her way to Miami on a crowded lifeboat stolen from a Havana dock. What she did have was a tight little ass she was willing to trade for the drugs she wanted.

"Hey, *cabrón*, we gonna do this or what?"

Pablo squeezed his eyes shut and kept tugging. "*Veta a la mierda*, Maria. You really not helping."

Maria regarded the half-erect dick in his hand, hoping that he wouldn't be able to perform at all. He was having more trouble than usual, addiction taking its toll on his cock and balls. The last few times he'd been inside her there was a definite lack of firmness. For all the tough posturing Pablo did around her, his floppy member was delicious irony. A chuckle crept up Maria's throat and threatened to pass her lips. She stifled it.

"*Me cago en Dios!*" Pablo seethed.

Things were taking too long, and Maria knew from experience that Pablo wouldn't give up the junk until he'd blown his load. To help things along she reached out and shooed his hands away, taking his cock in her fingers. She worked the shaft before slipping down to fondle his testicles.

"Put it in your mouth," Pablo whispered.

Maria glared at him. "No."

"C'mon, I showered today."

One sniff and Maria knew he was lying. She squeezed his cock hard to let him know that she wasn't impressed.

"No, Pablo."

The fierce grip excited him. She felt him grow inside her fist as moans of pleasure escaped his throat. She tugged more, making him grunt. When Pablo was as solid as he was going to get, he pushed Maria back and laid all of his weight on her, nestling his hips between her thighs, beer gut pushing on the flat of her belly. His skin was slick and oily. His rank breath produced sweat on her face.

"Don't take too long," Maria said.

He began pumping away, wheezing then moaning. Maria closed her eyes and tipped her head back so he would not try to kiss her. Halitosis stench blew on her throat instead. Even then, the wet heat of it made her squirm. It made her think about the boat trip from Cuba to America more than eight years before. Maria was sixteen when she became an illegal immigrant. Her virginity had been forcibly taken on that voyage by a deserting soldier with bad breath who never finished his journey with the rest. She thought about how their boat had departed from Cayo Coco with twelve people aboard and arrived in Florida with only eight. She remembered rations dwindling, drinking water running out. She remembered how no one came to her aid in the night when an uninvited man lay on top of her and muffled her cries. She recalled the accusations, the infighting, and the flashing of knives. She saw the bodies being thrown overboard.

"You like my cock, *chica*?" Pablo moaned, wanting some participation from her. "Do you love it?"

Maria gave two little groans to placate him before her thoughts returned to the lifeboat. The soldier hadn't asked Maria if she loved his cock, he demanded that she love it, ordering her to tell him how much with the hardest thrusts. After enduring two nights of him invading every orifice, Maria's first rapist also became her first victim. All it took was a knitting needle through the throat the moment his eyes were closed with orgasm.

"Oh, Maria," Pablo panted. "I think I'm going to come now. . . ."

The sound of footsteps came fast. Maria opened her eyes and saw a hand shoot out of the dark, entangling in her lover's greasy black hair. It pulled, wrenching Pablo's face upward and out of the light, his dick slipping from her as he went. He managed a squeal of protest before something muffled him. Maria could see the outlines of men in dark clothes surrounding her, Pablo struggling in the grip of one of them. She tried to rise and scream but another figure stepped forward and pressed a heavy boot against her neck, pinning her to the ground and cutting off her air.

"We're not taking him," she heard the man above her say. "Only the girl."

The figure holding Pablo kicked the back of his legs and dropped him to his knees. One of the others stepped forward and reached for something behind him. Maria didn't see the gun as it was drawn, but the muzzle flash lit up the alley for a moment, the loud retort a precursor to Pablo's right temple exploding in a spray of blood. His lifeless body teetered and fell forward, his face connecting with the pavement, nose breaking with a grisly crunch.

Maria whimpered prayers as the man standing on her neck leaned over and inspected her. She dared not look at him, but her nostrils picked up a familiar smell. It was the smell of cigars, undoubtedly Cuban, the kind that Castro and his army were fond of. Maria squirmed, tried to scream, but managed only a choke. She thought again of the lifeboat voyage and the soldier who pinned her against the gunwale as he tore at her clothes. The boot on her neck shifted and applied more weight to her jugular. Maria's eyes fluttered as her world dimmed. She let herself slip away without further struggle, knowing there was no escape.

Thirteen

NOW.

There was no escape. As evening approached that reality became obvious to everyone. Five of the six stranded reconvened around the trunk. They had all tried to eat, but ingested little. Ginger and Kenny picked at themselves, too busy scratching and pulling at scabs to take notice of anything around them. Maria sat, knees drawn up under her chin and arms wrapped around her shins like before, staring at the sand and mumbling prayers in Spanish. Nash and Felix gazed at the orange sunset, the sound of Maria's murmurings oddly soothing. The fireball at the sky's end was tamed enough by the dusk to look at for extended periods of time. Nash saw sunspots seared into his eyelids when he blinked.

"Beautiful," he whispered.

A gull cried out, drawing Nash's attention. Earlier, Felix had been chucking rocks at the birds puttering about the beach. Now they paddled offshore, well out of range. Nash watched the birds bobbing on the waves while Felix kept his eyes on the anchored yacht. It was impossible to tell if anyone was on deck in the fading light.

No one spoke for what seemed like ages. Despair came off each body like an odor. Only the sounds of scratching, coughing, or groaning were heard against the birdcalls and crashing waves. By the time Nash broke the silence, Tal had slunk his way back to the encampment like some kind of Gollum. He stayed well away from the others, squatting on the sand some thirty feet away.

"It's getting chilly out here," Nash said. "Wish they'd left us a frigging lighter or a box of matches so we could make a fire."

"They don't want us lighting any signal fires," replied Felix. "I'd have made us a big-ass bonfire already if I had an open flame."

Nash grunted in agreement, a sudden stab of pain in his stomach vetoing the words he was about to say. Rescue was growing more and more unlikely. Hope faded along with it. All day there had been no sign of anything other than the mysterious yacht.

"I'd set the whole damn island alight," Ginger said. "Burn everything in sight."

Felix rolled onto his knees and crawled to the open trunk. He looked inside and selected one of the sandwiches.

"You gonna eat your sandwich, Nash?"

Nash said nothing. His attention was fixed on a single gull riding the waves. It was alone, seemingly cast away from the others. The rest of the flock gave it a wide berth whenever it neared. Nash watched it with sympathy, thinking its solitary situation similar to his own. He wondered if it was diseased.

"Hey, let me know if you don't want this," Felix prodded. "'Cause I'll eat it instead if you care to donate."

Nash broke his gaze from the gull. He turned to Felix and put his hand up in a stopping gesture.

"Nah, I'll eat it eventually. I'm just waiting for this gut rot to pass—"

A loud squawk whipped Nash's attention back. In the orange glow he could see something dark rise out of the water, smooth and pointed, resembling the nose of a torpedo. It hit the underside of the gull and lifted it a foot before sliding back under the surface, dragging flapping white wings and open yellow beak with it. A fin or tail thrashed the water once as the gull disappeared.

Nash leapt to his feet. "Holy shit, did you see that?"

Felix and Maria were already looking at the spot. They hadn't seen half of what Nash had, but what they did glimpse was enough to give them both a sickened look of concern. Ginger and Kenny stopped picking at their skin and raised a pair of oblivious eyes: first to the water, then to Nash.

"What did you see?" Ginger asked.

"*Diablo,*" Maria whispered.

Nash and Felix exchanged a look. Felix shook his head in the slightest way, suggesting they not expand on the topic. Nash agreed. No reason to scare anyone more than they already were. The lie came out slowly. A reversal of what had transpired.

"Gull caught a fish," he mustered. "Snagged a big one too. Impressive."

Ginger snorted. "Jeez, it don't take much to entertain you, does it?"

The grit in her voice was sandpaper on Nash's nerves. An itch on his chest caught the savage scratch he wanted to rake across her face. She went back to picking at her scabs and Nash fantasized about kicking sand in her mouth.

"Fuck off, carrottop," Nash said, wrapping his arms around his shivering self. "Not much to entertain any of us on this goddamn lump of land."

"You could benefit from a little rest and relaxation."

"What I could benefit from is a fucking fix."

Nash's pain and frustration were compounding every

hour now. All he could think about was a hit, needing a needle in him like a nymphomaniac needed hard dick. Desperation burrowed deeper into his inner dark, trying to avoid being dragged out into the light. It wouldn't be long before he lashed out at someone.

"Those gulls have the right idea," Kenny said. "We'll have to catch fish ourselves soon, once we run out of this here food."

"There's more food on the next island," Felix replied.

Kenny's eyes bulged. "That's crazy talk, man."

Kenny looked around at the rest, expecting sounds and signs of agreement. They avoided eye contact. No one said a word.

"Right?" said Kenny, wide eyes unblinking. "We're not going to try anything as stupid as that, right, guys?"

Nash shrugged. "Look, I'm not saying it's not stupid—"

A flurry of dull thumps suddenly pounded the sand. The five turned in the direction of the running footsteps, hearing the last few beats on the beach before the splashing started through the shallows. Nash knew what was happening before he laid eyes on it.

"Oh, shit."

Everyone scrambled to their feet and made an unbalanced run in the direction of the commotion, stumbling as they went.

"Tal!" Ginger cried. "Stop!"

"What the hell does he think he's doing?" Felix seethed.

Tal charged into the surf, legs pulling him awkwardly through the water, arms stroking the air as if helping to propel him forward. Running steps soon became lurches as the water deepened. Everyone yelled for his return, Felix's voice bellowing over the others.

"What the fuck is wrong with you?"

"He is crazed," Maria said, making the sign of the cross. "His head is sick. He gives in to his demon now."

"Don't do it, Tal!" Nash yelled. "It's too dangerous!"

Felix ran after him, getting as far as the shallows. "Get back here, you crazy son of a bitch. You'll never make it!"

Tal toppled into the water, churning it frothy with his limbs, fighting against the current. The others ran helplessly to the water's edge.

"It's suicide," said Ginger.

Tal wasn't listening to a word. The evening light was fading fast. The five onshore yelled again and again, watching in disbelief as Tal stroked his way farther out under the remaining orange hue. Soon he was only a dark bump riding the waves, growing more and more difficult to track with every passing moment.

"He's a goner," groaned Felix.

He turned and walked back to the trunk. Everyone

followed except Nash. He continued to watch long after he had lost sight of Tal in the fading light, eyes and ears straining for any sign of the man, hoping maybe he would come to his senses and swim back. He waited until the sun finally sank below the horizon, dragging the last of the day's glow down the side of the planet, leaving him in gloom.

"Godspeed, Tallahassee, you lunatic."

Nash shuffled back to the others, head hung in defeat. They all took a side around the trunk and lay down. The cool air of emerging night breezed over their bodies, causing them to curl up like flowers in the dark. Quiet descended, the sound of crashing waves continuing their rhythm in the background, interrupted only by the odd cough or groan. Tension and frustration came off each person with an invisible heat. Horrible thoughts collided in their minds, jarring nerves with every hit, their needs and fears wrestling for control.

In time they settled as exhaustion took hold. The silence implied deep slumber, but Nash figured the others just stared at the stars above like he did. For the first time in years he felt afraid of the dark. He would have been thankful for it, though, had he known what it concealed from them that night. Out in the channel, near the spot where Nash had lost track of Tal, the water was clouded red with blood.

Hours later, at the far end of the island, near where

a madman had perched on his rock, something ragged and gray washed ashore. Not much was left of Tallahassee Jones in the small hours of the morning. Just his torso connected to what remained of his left arm. It was almost unidentifiable, the bloodless upper body flopping back and forth on the wet sand with each incoming wave like some oversized, half-eaten jellyfish. His appendage was cut to ribbons, only the index finger and thumb left unscathed. Large concave bites cut the corpse off below the sternum, open wounds exposing rib cage and spine. Tal's jaw and bottom row of teeth sat atop a broken neck. Everything else had been eaten away.

Something large thrashed the shallow water fifty feet from the remains, wanting desperately to get closer, to finish off what it had started.

Fourteen

There was unfinished business, Nash was sure of it. Not all of his fuckups had been forgiven. Not all of his debts had been paid. Someone had snitched for one reason or another and now the cops were on to him. No doubt they were serious about it too. If they were coming down to his level like this, then they had hopes of making a trophy out of his head. For the moment Nash was still a step ahead, though it was clear the narcs knew he was in the nightclub. They scanned the crowd thoroughly, trying to acquire their target, noses in the air like wolves with a scent.

There were two of them this time. Same blond guy from the supermarket a couple days earlier, and someone new who was undoubtedly backup. They looked eerily similar. Same build, height, and demeanor—a

115

pair of stone-cold soldiers on a mission. They didn't blend into the crowd. Stoic faces and rigid postures made them easy marks. Nash had no problem keeping tabs on them.

He kept watch from behind a pillar on the club's second-floor overlook. It was a good spot, easy to duck out of sight should they raise their eyes. Strobe lights, smoke machines, and shadowed recesses provided more cover if Nash needed it, though he wondered how much longer he could evade them. At any moment they would stop looking and start searching. Nash was sure he'd get caught up in their sweep of the place.

He checked his pockets again, making sure he was clean. Every pill and packet had been flushed after he caught his first glimpse of the blond guy. Ecstasy, ketamine, Percs, and poppers all down the toilet. But looking at the two operatives now, seeing their focus and intent, Nash didn't think ridding himself of the contraband was going to get him off the hook. They weren't here for his drugs. They were here for him. Probably had a warrant they'd been looking to execute for a while. He had to make himself scarce.

Back exit again? he thought. *Double my luck?*

No. They'd be wise to it after the supermarket escape. Walking right out the front door, however, might be the last thing they'd expect. Nash scrutinized the dance floor below, looking for a third operative, a possible sleeper in the crowd. Through the multicolored flashes and thin haze, none of the sweating bodies clad in casual night attire struck him as suspicious. If there was a sleeper, he was well disguised. The two on the ground floor began to move out. Nash weighed his options.

Whatever you do, don't get your ass backed into a corner.

These guys were the better-trained pigs, possibly even a task force. It was only a matter of time before they found him. Nash decided to try to flee the building while he still had the jump on them. Getting past unnoticed would be a challenge.

I need to change things up.

Nash looked over his shoulder at the second-floor bar. Standing at the far end was a lone dude in his mid-twenties wearing a fedora and a checkered shirt over a wife-beater, bopping his head to the dance beat with too much enthusiasm. The same guy had bought two tabs of E and a popper off Nash an hour earlier. Nash sized him up, figured they were about the same height and weight. He made his way over, pulling out his wallet and counting out some of his ill-gotten gains. The dude saw him coming and grinned, teeth clenched.

"Hey, man," Nash said. "That stuff treating you well?"

Dude nodded vigorously. "Hell yeah, bro, feeling great. Thanks for the hookup. You're the man."

Nash smiled. "Glad you like it. Listen, I got a little proposition for you."

The dude's eyes became confused, then wary. The grin remained even though he folded his arms and took a step backward.

"Sorry, bud, I don't swing that way."

Nash laughed. "No, no, dude. It's nothing like that. Look, I dig your style. You got a sharp eye for fashion. What would you say if I gave you fifty bucks to trade my shirt for yours plus the hat?"

"Fifty bucks?"

The dude looked at him cockeyed. Nash shrugged and showed him the two twenties and ten folded in his fingers. Dude's grin widened. He took off the hat and placed it on Nash's head.

"I'd say you got yourself a deal, man."

Nash tucked the cash in the breast pocket of his shirt and traded it. The checkered short-sleeve was a snug fit over his white tee, but the hat was made to measure. He pulled the brim down low and shook the dude's hand.

"Thanks, you've made my day."

"Bro, you've made *my* day."

Dude chuckled and unexpectedly gave him a hug, Ecstasy affectionate. Nash headed back to his spot behind the pillar and looked out over the dance floor again. One of the narcs was mounting the stairs to the second floor. The other was pacing along the main bar, searching the crowd of dancers. Nash waited, hiding in plain sight, watching from the corner of his eye as the first narc reached the second floor and scanned the customers. Nash made sure he kept out of his line of sight.

"Take the bait," Nash muttered.

Between the moving bodies, something of interest caught the narc's eye. The dude at the bar was ordering another drink with his back turned. The narc advanced slowly on the decoy. Nash swept around and got behind unnoticed, then slipped down the stairs behind a trio of men that he did his best to blend in with.

Once on the ground floor, Nash dissolved into the dance floor. He pushed his way through the packed crowd until he reached the front doors, expecting a strong hand to land on his shoulder at any moment and shove him to the ground. At the club's entrance he turned and took one last look inside. The first narc was at the pillar where Nash had been, signaling to his counterpart below that their target had not been found. Nash backed up, eyes fixed on his enemies, the small of his back depressing the door's lock bar with a clunk.

Outside, the cool night sucked at the stale air bottled within the nightclub, pulling Nash onto the sidewalk faster than he was expecting to go. He stumbled off the curb and almost fell into traffic. A cab laid on its horn, berating him for being a drunken idiot. Nash waved a middle finger in the air.

"Squat and spin on it, dickhead!" he yelled.

"Chill out, man," someone behind him said.

Nash shut his mouth. It was foolish, drawing attention like that. People nearby were regarding him distastefully over his outburst. He shrugged and gave an innocent grin. All eyes quickly tired of him and fell away. Nash adjusted his hat and began walking. The clicking sound of high heels on pavement came to his ears, but he kept his head down and shoulders hunched, trying to quicken his step without making it obvious. His mind protested.

Quit dragging your heels and hightail it already.

His gut disagreed. Running was a mistake. He'd cleared the club without incident. Now he had to casually put some distance between it and himself. A second cab honked at him, two short pips, sussing him out for a fare. Nash flagged the yellow car down. Nearby, the clicking sound sped up. He opened the back door and slipped in, his elbow digging into the person who had unexpectedly entered the cab from the other side.

"Ow!" she exclaimed, rubbing her arm. "Fucking hell . . ."

"Hey, get your own damn cab—"

Nash turned to regard his uninvited companion as she pushed back a long lock of black hair and eyed him challengingly. He was immediately disarmed. She was maybe twenty-five with pale skin and pouting lips, smoking body in blue jeans and tight black tee, rating an eight out of ten in Nash's book. There was a hint of wear and tear on her, but nothing he couldn't smooth out if he played his cards right.

"Sorry," he said. "I thought I had this one to myself."

She wasn't impressed. "That makes two of us."

They had a standoff. Neither of them moved an inch. The cabdriver watched irritably from the rearview mirror. Nash took off his hat and made a show of locking his door.

"Look, honey, ordinarily I'd be a gentleman and let you take this one and wait for another, but tonight ain't an ordinary night. I really, really need this cab."

"Where do you need to get to so bad?"

"Just can't be here right now, that's all. Sooner I'm gone the better."

The girl gave a thoughtful pause, held his eyes, and didn't budge. The driver turned in his seat and spoke in a gruff, impatient voice.

"I ain't got all night. Where to, mister?"

"Take me east."

"I'm going east too," said the girl. "You wanna . . . ride partway together? Maybe split the fare?"

Nash's smile was sly. "Works for me."

o o o

Across town, Ginger Rosen was sitting on Curtis Moffat's couch, putting a much-needed needle to vein. The apartment was a mess, fast-food containers strewn

121

about, empty beer cans on every flat surface, cigarette butts overflowing from ashtrays onto the floor, where they caught in the shag carpet and were crushed underfoot. Curtis was in the next room negotiating another of his business ventures, leaving Ginger to get high alone. Whatever had him tied up on the phone was important enough to miss out on a hit. Ginger didn't know and didn't want to know. He'd been moody since she'd shown up on his doorstep an hour earlier looking to score.

"Come to Momma, you little prick."

She was overdue for it. The needle trembled slightly in her hand, trying to find a vein beneath the belt that tied off her bicep. She pierced her skin and depressed the plunger on the syringe while singing a lick of Rick James.

"Give me your stuff, that funk, that sweet, that funky stuff."

The sweet, the funk, the illicit stuff infused with her blood, attaching to receptors, swallowing her biochemistry in a warm, satin-lined mouth. A hit hadn't been this good or strong in years. Felt like she was having her cherry popped for the first time.

"Ohhh, give it to me, baby . . ."

Ginger trailed off into mumbles, the junk disabling her finer functions as it bloomed inside her. Right here, spoon cooked and syringe shot, this was her lover, her partner, her angel and demon rolled into one. She didn't know where Curtis was scoring his shit from, but she was determined not to go back to anything less pure. If there was a God who gifted paradise to those made in his image, then this brand of heroin was surely the sample. It gave her a glimpse through the very gates of heaven. If only she could find a way to chain herself to them, then she might feel blessed again.

Curtis came out from the bedroom, cell phone in hand. He sat next to Ginger on the sofa, distracted, distant. Ginger reached out and caressed his arm, fingertips seeming to connect with every individual blond hair on his tanned skin.

"This stuff you scored is sooooo good, baby."

Curtis pulled his arm away and refused to look at her, expelling a breath of aggravated air that turned into a cough. When he spoke his tone was unusually quiet, thoughtful.

"Yeah, you dig it?"

"Uh-fucking-huh. I think it's the best I ever shot."

"It's that good, eh?"

"Oh, yeah, you gotta try and get this shit for us all the time."

"Right," Curtis snorted. "You gonna pay for your share of it if I do?"

The sudden curtness in his voice pinched Ginger. She tried to crease her brow, feign a pout. The slack muscles in her face didn't respond well. She made her voice as pitiful as she could instead.

"Baby . . . I . . . I ain't got no money right now, baby."

Curtis did look at her then. There wasn't an ounce of empathy in his eyes, though something else swam in the blue irises. To Ginger it looked like guilt, but she didn't understand why that would be.

"You never have any fucking money, Ginger," he grumbled, sounding oddly defensive. "I can't even remember the last time you went out and grabbed for us."

"Baby—"

"Don't 'baby' me, for Christ's sake!" he snapped. "I doubt you'd even stay with me if I didn't hook you up on a regular basis."

Curtis rose and went to the kitchen to fix a drink. Ginger didn't know what was upsetting him, but figured it had more to do with the phone call than any money she owed. Her own emotions were smothered under the weight of the junk. She couldn't duel with him in such a state.

"Don't be like that," she moaned.

Curtis poured a straight scotch. "Don't be like what?"

"Don't be all mad at me and shit. I ain't done nothing except lie here and stay out of your way tonight."

"All you ever do is lie the fuck around, Ginger."

There was a marked downshift in her drugged delight. "C'mon, I don't want to fight, baby. I'll pay you back next time I have it."

Curtis laughed. "And when would that be?"

Ginger went quiet. Truth was, she didn't know. Even if she did, both of them knew it would be a cold day in hell before she'd cough it up for dope already consumed. Curtis leaned against the kitchen counter and threw back a mouthful from his tumbler.

"The world runs on money, sweetheart. You get that, don't you? Everything has a price; nothing in life is free. Here I am, paying the rent, paying the bills, buying the groceries, supporting both your ass and your habit. I got fucking debt, Ginger, and lots of it too. What are you bringing to the table?"

Another downshift and her euphoria was first gear all over again. Ginger worried her high would get stuck in reverse if Curtis kept up his attack.

"Fuck, why are you being like this?" she snarled. "You're totally ruining my high."

That look slipped again onto Curtis's face, something guilty, something worried in his eyes. Ginger turned and buried her face in a pillow, playing up the sad act, hoping to make him come to her. In no time she felt his weight sink into the cushions beside her.

"I'm sorry," he said. "You do bring something to the table."

Ginger's muffled voice was little more than a moan. "What?"

Curtis paused, leaning over to massage her shoulders until she turned her pout toward him. He looked into her eyes and tried to smile, brushing back strands of hair from her forehead.

"You."

He kissed her then, gently, awkwardly. There was something boyish and scared about it, but the kiss was enough of a gesture. She rose as he withdrew his lips, draping a leg over his lap to straddle him.

"You want me to do you?" she said, biting her bottom lip dreamily.

Curtis raised an eyebrow. "Are you referring to the drugs or my dick?"

"Whatever you want, baby. I'm game for either."

Another attempt to smile, followed by a shake of his head. Ginger raised both eyebrows in surprise. It wasn't like Curtis to turn down a fuck from her. Not like him at all. She rode his lap and jiggled her rack to try to coax something more positive out of him. He patted her ass nonchalantly, showing his utter lack of interest.

"Not right now, babe, I wanna keep my head straight. I've still got some things to take care of tonight."

Ginger was curious for the first time. "Who was that on the phone, anyway?"

"Just business." Curtis shrugged and glanced at his

watch. "Someone's coming around later to pick some-thing up."

His irises gave up nothing more, and Ginger knew better than to ask him further about his affairs. With all the pies Curtis was plunging fingers into lately, the less Ginger knew the better. The topic of a certain little slut wasn't off-limits, however.

"Rita's not coming by, is she?"

Curtis shook his head vehemently. "No, don't worry."

"Good, I hate that skank."

Curtis braced for some Rita bashing. Ginger let the topic slide, incapable of giving two shits about much. The heroin had her in far too pleasant a mood and there was plenty of time to hate on Rita later.

"Look, I'm sorry I got shitty with you," Curtis said. "I didn't mean to bring you down, especially during your high. Let me make it up to you."

"Baby, this dope already makes up for anything and everything. You're off the hook for the foreseeable future."

She grinned lazily, slinging rubbery arms around his neck. He put a firm hand under her ass and eased her off his lap so he could rise.

"Regardless, I'm gonna fix you a drink."

Curtis returned to the kitchen and prepared some-thing on the counter with his back to her. Ginger sprawled on the sofa and stared at the stucco ceiling, a grin stretched across her face, not a care in the world. She felt suspended above the cushions, as if her body had been hollowed out and filled with warm helium. To her the stucco looked like the soft, creamy tips of Cool Whip. She saw herself floating up off the couch to run her tongue over a ceiling of dessert, dip hands into its cool, buttery texture, write words with a finger in its white surface.

I could write my life story in that, she thought. *I could . . .*

And suddenly there it was, clear as day in the center of her head, a worm wriggling and writhing with both pleasure and pain. If she could reach inside her brain it would be cool and smooth to the touch, slithering around her finger, then arm, then body. Ginger danced with the worm.

I'll wrap you around my brain stem and tie you in a knot so you can never leave.

She felt weight sink into the cushions beside her again. Curtis had come back, and he'd brought something with him.

"Here," Curtis said, handing her a mug. "Drink this."

"What is it?" she mumbled, returning to her senses.

"Something to help your high along, make it twice as good."

Ginger took the mug and drank every last drop. It was syrupy sweet, but a bitter aftertaste drizzled on the back of her tongue.

"Tastes weird," she said. "What liquor did you use . . . ?"

She felt time and space around her stretch, sights and sounds warping, her world collapsing into a bloated, lethargic state. Curtis was saying something, but his voice was a series of deep yawns, foreign and frightening. Ginger closed her eyes, waiting for her high to grow exponentially. Soon paradise was lost completely and darkness came.

o o o

An hour later, Felix Fenton was climbing the stairwell to his apartment off of Seventy-ninth Street. The ascent felt like a hike up a mountainside in cement shoes. His movements were sluggish, feet dragging, toes catching on the lip of every stair. Walking straight was proving a challenge. The wall and the banister bounced his staggering body between them. Drool leaked from the corner of his mouth. His breath stunk of booze, his head lost in the haze of a hit. There was a worm inside his brain, a wonderful wiggly worm that danced to the beat of his heart. A car stereo, boosted from an unlocked car in a quiet lot, swung by his side in a plastic shopping bag. Felix intended to fence it in the morning to fund his next grab.

An hour earlier Felix had needed his hit so bad he'd asked to shoot up in the apartment of Al Catraz mere seconds after buying. The drug dealer had reluctantly permitted him to cook a quick spoon in his kitchen, on condition that Felix make himself scarce as soon as he was fixed. Felix wanted to kick back, sink into an armchair, and enjoy his junk, but he knew better than to piss off a supplier. He took to the street after injection and headed home in a daze. Catraz wasn't the closest drug dealer by a long shot, but the cat was rumored to be selling shit of such quality it was worth the long walk to his neighborhood. The rumors were true. The junk coursing through Felix's veins was of a variety rarely seen, let alone sampled, in his neck of the woods.

Felix finally reached the third floor and lumbered down the hallway to his apartment door, where he stabbed his key repeatedly above the door handle, trying to penetrate the lock.

"Fucking fuck," he mumbled. "Open, damn it."

He leaned against the door, trying to focus. A half dozen more jabs and the key slipped in, disengaging the lock. Felix turned and pushed back the knob. The black beyond it surprised him, thick and foreign and cool. The worm in his head stopped wiggling for a moment.

"What the . . . ?"

Darkness filled every inch of the apartment. Felix didn't know why. He was sure he'd left a light or two on. Leaving lights on was a bad habit he'd had since childhood. Lights on had kept the boogeyman in his closet away, the monster under the bed away, and sometimes the drunken fists of his stepfather away. Felix couldn't remember the last time he'd returned to a blacked-out crib. He remained standing in the hallway, unsure of whether to enter, wishing he could gather his wits about him. The heroin and whiskey created a solid buffer.

"Damn junk," he grumbled. "Damned *junkie*."

For a moment he despised the narcotic within him, wishing he could fight it off the way he'd fought off so many opponents in the ring as a young man, wishing it had a physical form so he could plant a digger in the gut and bring it to its knees. The bookies had always given him a one-in-four chance of winning. As a kid, he had the same likelihood of catching a beating from his mother's poor taste in men. Felix never liked those odds. He'd done his damnedest to be king underdog. If smack was a heavyweight contender Felix would have it tangled in the ropes and hammered into submission.

"Jesus, what did you expect, Felix? You beat him to a bloody pulp."

Felix remembered the angry, ashamed words spewing from Sheldon Monet's mouth. They were almost two decades old now, but his former manager's words rang as clear as they had in the locker room after Felix's fateful bout in the ring.

"You couldn't exercise a little restraint out there? Fuck,

what did I expect? That's how you were trained. Like a god-damn pit bull."

That night Felix had sat on a bench and said nothing, knowing he was finished. Sheldon wasn't close to being finished, however. Spittle flew off his lips as he continued to berate him. Felix took the verbal beating in silence while his trainer toweled off the sweat from his body and cut his wraps.

"You can't be controlled. You're a loose cannon, ticking time bomb, and rabid animal all rolled into one. And you wanna know something else, you fucking caveman? I can't defend your ignorant ass anymore. I'm gonna have a hard enough time defending myself from—"

As soon as the wraps fell, Felix decked his manager with bare knuckles and watched Sheldon's front teeth sail through the air, lit by fluorescent light, and clatter off an old locker. Sheldon staggered into a corner, hands over his mouth, blood seeping through fingers. He tried to find purchase on the brick wall before collapsing in a heap. Felix was heading for the door before his manager even hit the floor.

"I'm done," Felix had said, picking up his gym bag. "For good."

His trainer, severed wraps in hand, begged him to reconsider, but Felix never boxed another day in his life.

"Wasn't my fault," Felix mumbled.

He'd said it then, and he was saying it again now. For close to twenty years he'd repeated this mantra that did him no good. He'd walked away from a fucked-up fight and into a personal hell, out of the frying pan and into the fire. Hell, for all its fiery depictions, was more likely to be found on the earth's crust rather than below it. Now, as he stood in front of his apartment, he couldn't help but feel the doorway before him was the entrance to some other hell. It was ridiculous, of course, being as high and drunk as he was, but he couldn't shake the vibe. To prove the feeling wrong, Felix strode defiantly into the dark.

Five feet inside the doorway he stopped. There was a shuffling sound at his back, rubber soles beginning to move across the floorboards. He felt a presence emerge from behind the door a second before it snaked an arm around his neck and put him in a choke hold. A jacketed bicep and forearm flexed against Felix's throat, the power of the squeeze almost superhuman. He thought his neck would break, but only his lungs were denied air. Felix recognized the Texas drawl the second the voice spoke in his ear.

"Now today . . . today just *ain't* your lucky day."

The elbow inclined, lifting Felix's chin. The pierce of a needle, something Felix knew well, immediately stung the flesh of his exposed neck. The bagged car stereo dropped to the ground with a clunk. Felix struggled, but his assailant maintained the strong hold easily. His body began to go limp as his vision blurred. The silhouettes of the furniture in the apartment swayed and swirled before his eyes. Felix was out before he hit the floor.

o o o

Miles away in Overtown, two men were loading Kenny Colbert's unconscious body into a gray windowless GMC van parked in the alley behind Matty and Merle's place. Merle was in the alley too, arguing with the men who had come to collect. They didn't answer many of his questions or respond to any of his demands. Merle didn't like the way things were being handled. He didn't think things were fair. He wanted to alter the deal.

One of the men, after hearing Merle out, made a call on his cell phone. The voice on the other end first listened, and then gave instructions. When the call was complete the man conferred quietly with the other. It had been decided that M&M had exhausted their usefulness. Things in the alley went very, very quiet.

"Hey, wait a second," Merle whined as one of the men advanced on him. "What do you think you're doing?"

There was a click. The man swung at him, hand at neck level. Merle barely saw it coming. The switchblade that slit his throat nixed the scream before it could escape. A wretched, gargled sound spilled from his mouth instead, blood following it out. Merle fell first to his knees and then flat on his face. His assailant stood over his twitching body and watched as he bled out. The other man went back into the apartment and searched room to room until he found Matty cowering in the bathtub, intoxicated and in tears. For all of his slender build, Matty managed to struggle with his attacker for almost a minute before his throat was cut.

Part Two

TRIPPING

Fifteen

Dawn was breaking when the voices stirred Nash from his painful slumber. He'd spent the night in a fetal position in an attempt to quell the stabbing in his stomach, but it hadn't helped much. He'd managed a little sleep, much the same as he would get with a fever: restless, with frequent spells of cold sweat and confusion. Felix's rumbling baritone and Ginger's high-pitched squeak forced Nash to give up on the prospect of any further rest, yet he continued to lie still, face turned away just enough to watch them without their knowledge.

"So where was you, last you remember?" asked Felix. "Y'know, before you woke up here?"

"Lying on my so-called boyfriend's couch," said Ginger.

"Boyfriend?"

"Boyfriend, roommate, dealer, call him what you want."

"I thought you was a dyke."

"Never said I was."

Felix gave a little cackle at the revelation. A low wolf whistle followed. Ginger made a noise halfway between a snort and a giggle and shook her head.

"You wish, buddy."

Felix chuckled. "Hey, you know what they say. Once you go black—"

Ginger didn't miss a beat. "You might get stabbed."

Felix stared at her, jaw slack, momentarily speechless. Then he threw his head back and let out a hoot of laughter.

"Ice *cold*, lady."

Ginger chuckled. "Believe it or not, that's just me warming up to you."

"Alright, so you were on your boyfriend's couch and then . . . ?"

"Dunno, passed out after my hit, I guess. Next thing I know I'm waking up here with the rest of you guys."

Felix shook his head. "It wasn't the junk that put you out. Whatever we all got drugged with was meant to keep us under for a good while. The last thing I remember was coming back to my apartment and putting my key in the door. I was out of it, drunk and dazed from a spoonful, but I thought I heard something behind me. I remember an instance of pain . . . then nothing. Pretty sure I got injected with something."

Ginger nodded, but said nothing. If she was going to admit to being drugged like Felix, then she'd have to admit that Curtis might have had something to do with it. Felix turned to an exhausted, but wide-eyed, Kenny.

"What 'bout you, kid?"

"I was at a friend's place. These guys I hang with, Merle and Matty, hooked me up with a fix and I remember sitting in an armchair staring at the TV. First time I'd ever done intravenous."

Felix laughed. "Never needled? Shit, son, you hardly qualify as a junkie."

"I freebased a fuckload to make up for it, but I'll never go back now. I learned what I was missing out on when Matty pumped me full of that bliss. Last thing I remember was Merle fixing me a bowl of ice cream. I ate it in front of the TV as I started to come down. Something about it tasted funny. . . ."

"So you guys were with other people, last you remember . . . and people you knew. And you were also in the middle of your last hit."

Kenny and Ginger nodded reluctantly, not liking what it was adding up to.

"What about him over there?" Kenny said, thumbing toward Nash's supposedly sleeping figure. "What's his story?"

Nash didn't move an inch, but his response startled everyone.

"I went to bed with a devil woman."

"Haven't we all?" Felix said and looked at Ginger and Kenny. "Present company excepted, of course."

"Had my share," said Ginger with a shrug and turned to Nash. "You've been awake this whole time?"

"Fuck," Nash groaned. "With you bunch yakking away there's no way I could be anything else."

He sat up on his elbows, blinking in the morning light. His attention was drawn to Maria. She sat away from the others, staring silently at the sunrise with bloodshot eyes. Nash didn't feel much like talking himself, but Felix wanted to hear more.

"Alright, so who's this devil woman? And what's she got to do with anything?"

"Nothing," Nash replied. "Or everything. I don't know. She was the last person I was with before ending up here."

"How well do you know her?"

"I don't. Never met her before in my life."

Nash put his hand down the front of his jeans and gave his balls a good scratch while he collected his thoughts. Ginger grimaced at the sight.

"Aw, have an ounce of class, man."

Nash ignored her. "Two nights ago I'm at a club in Opa-locka, dealing the odd party favor, when I catch sight of two guys that look out of place on the dance floor. It takes me a moment to realize that I've seen one of these fuckers before, a couple days before in a supermarket. At the time I was convinced that the guy was tailing me. Something about him screamed *cop*. I thought the narcs had got wind of me somehow and I figured they were setting up a trap, so I bolted out a back exit and hightailed it."

"They come after you?" Kenny asked.

"I didn't give them the chance. I head to my apartment to lie low, take my medicine, and forget about the whole thing in a day. But I'm back out the next night, and lo and behold, this same guy is in the club. Except this time he's got backup."

"Only two guys?" Felix asked. "Seems a little light for a vice squad."

"I thought so too, but I'm sure it was just the two of them. They looked the part, and they were both on the hunt, no doubt."

"So what did you do?"

"First, I went into the can and flushed all the shit I had on me. Then I managed to give them the slip and get out of the club. Outside I hailed a cab, but some hot young thing comes out of nowhere and gets in the car the same time I do. She asks where I'm headed. I tell her I'm going east and she suggests we split a fare. Short on cash and out of product, I don't object. In the cab we get to chatting. She invites me along for a little barhopping and I'm game. She's crazy, no doubt, but the kind of ride you really wanna strap yourself into. We get hammered and I find out she's more of a dope fiend than I am, so I roll with the punches until I end up at her place for a fuck and a fix. Right after we finish doing the nasty she admits she's a fan."

"What do you mean a fan?" asked Ginger.

"A fan of the band. She'd been to a bunch of Fuel Injector gigs . . . although I don't ever remember seeing her."

"Then what?"

"Got high, got sleepy, and the next thing I know I'm waking up here with you lot . . . fucked in a whole other way."

Felix nodded. "Ain't that the truth."

"Which begs the question," Nash said, sitting cross-legged on the sand. "You guys notice anything suspicious? I mean . . . earlier that day or the days before? Anything out of the ordinary?"

There was pause for thought, but it didn't take long for Ginger to break it.

"Yeah, some weird shit happened to me at the Barracuda Room. This guy was hounding me at the bar, trying real hard to get me back to his place. Good-looking dude, built like an army boy, sounded like a New Yorker. At first I was kinda flattered. Thought he might be a sailor in port with a little shore leave, looking for a good time. Said he could hook me up with anything I wanted if I just went home with him."

"You take him up on his offer?" Felix asked.

"Nah, something didn't feel right. His vibe was off, too intense, too pushy. I've been around the block. I know what shit smells like, no matter how much cologne is dumped on it. Figured he was either a sicko or a psycho, and I didn't want to find out which. So I ditched him first chance I got."

"Did he try and follow you?" Nash asked.

"Like you, I didn't even give him the chance. Told him I was going to powder my beak and blew out the Barracuda the second I saw he was distracted."

Nash scratched the inside of his arm. "If there's one thing our kind knows how to do well, it's run and hide."

Felix folded fingers into fists. "Not me."

"Not you?"

Felix shook his head. Ginger snuck a glance at his hands, noting the prominent scar tissue and bony knuckles. She didn't doubt the kind of damage they could inflict.

"You attack your problems, don't you?"

"Fight or flight," Felix said, nodding. "I choose fight."

"You got a story too?"

"Yeah, I came home to find some piece of shit snooping around my apartment door a couple days back."

"Good-looking guy?" asked Ginger.

Felix let out a snort. "How the hell would I know?"

"I'm just trying to draw some connections here. Wondering if it was the same guy I had hitting on me in that bar."

"Nah, this guy talked like a cowboy, a real fucking hick. When I approached him he tried to flee the scene. He took a swing at me when I got within arm's reach. I ducked the punch and tried to go toe-to-toe with him. Only managed to land one blow and it didn't even faze the cocksucker."

"Tough guy, eh?" said Nash.

"*Trained* guy," Felix replied. "There's a difference. This son of a bitch had moves, man. Before I knew it he had me in a clinch and planted a couple of knees in my gut, dropping me like a fucking amateur. Thought he was going to finish the job, but he said it was my lucky day and walked off, leaving me winded on the floor."

The others traded troubled looks. Someone taking down Felix so easily was hard to imagine after seeing the man's penchant for violence and aggression firsthand.

Kenny raised a hand. "I think I'm in the same boat.

I saw a stranger hanging around in the lobby of my apartment, now that you got me thinking."

"You too?" Felix asked. "When?"

"Two, maybe three days ago. I can't really remember. But I do remember him clearly. He was well-built. Cropped blond hair, handsome—"

Kenny caught himself smiling at the thought, forgetting where he was for a moment. He looked around guiltily at the others.

Nash snorted. "Don't worry, kid. You ain't a mystery to us."

"Got *fag* written all over you," Felix said. "No offense, man."

"Oh, none taken," Kenny said, rolling his eyes.

An uncomfortable silence followed, all three men not knowing how to continue the conversation. Ginger finally spoke up, trying to draw attention away from Kenny and put an end to the idiocy.

"Maria, what about you? Care to share?"

Maria said nothing. She was looking out at the water, making herself an island by staying away from the rest. Ginger didn't press her for an answer. It was clear the woman wanted to keep to herself.

"Cat got her tongue?" Felix asked.

"Leave her be," Ginger replied. "I've heard enough already anyway."

"You got a theory?"

"Hardly, but from what you guys have told me it sounds to me like we all had the same people tailing us. Match that with the fact that we're all dope fiends, and I'd say we were picked out, targeted. Don't know why or how, but we were in someone's crosshairs for sure."

"Or maybe we're the dumb luck of the draw?" said Nash. "Six short straws?"

"Five now," said Ginger.

Nash nodded. "Yeah . . ."

He scraped at his scarred forearms, wondering how life might have panned out if he'd never tried that first hit backstage three dates into his one and only East Coast tour. Ginger watched, knowing he had the worse habit between them, but only by a small margin. She glanced at her own skin, thinking how soft and unblemished it could have been if she'd never got into the habit of sticking herself.

"I will tell you this, though," said Nash. "What that mystery girl cooked up for me was the best junk I ever had."

"Come again?" Ginger said, snapping into focus.

"If my last hit was my last meal, it would have been some serious gourmet shit. The high was unbelievable. Felt like the first time again. Felt like I had this wonderful worm inside my head, just wriggling, dancing."

Eyes widening, Ginger pointed a finger at herself. "Me too."

"Me too," said Kenny.

Felix raised a hand. "Same here."

"No shit, who supplies you?" Nash asked.

"Recently, I been grabbing from this guy named Al Catraz," Felix replied.

"Al Catraz?"

"Yeah, his street name. You know him?"

"No. Why they call him that?"

"They say the guy is an island," Felix said. "Nobody can get to him. He's careful, smart, been dealing for years and never done a day inside. He's never had as much as a parking ticket either, so I hear."

Nash turned to Kenny. "What about you?"

"I get my shit from Matty and Merle mostly," Kenny said. "Once in a while I'll grab off a corner."

"And you?" Nash asked Ginger.

"My boyfriend, Curtis, hooks me up. And recently he's been bringing home exactly what you said, that wonderful, wiggly worm stuff."

A subtle smile curled the corners of her mouth. She looked at them all and discovered they wore similar expressions.

Nash shook his head in disbelief. "Jesus, I think we were all scoring the same dope somehow."

"I wonder . . ." Felix began, looking out to the island across the channel.

"What?"

"I wonder if that's the same heroin they got waiting for us over there. Wonder if our last high was just a taste."

Nash nodded. "That thought crossed my mind too."

The idea was appetizing. Even Maria looked back at the mention of it. The five shared a look of increased interest.

"God, I'd love me just one little hit of that bomb shit right now," Felix said.

"Tell me about it—"

A sharp pain cut across the inside of Nash's gut, doubling him over with a hiss. The others grew worried. Their conversation had been uncharacteristically calm, but they knew it wouldn't last. It was plain to see, on each of their faces, the lines of stress, shifty eyes, twitching lips. They could only stave off the inevitable for so long. This crazy train they were riding, the same unstable locomotion that drove Tal out to sea some ten hours earlier, could only go off the tracks. The real cracks would appear soon in their psyche. Cold turkey was, in fact, not really an option. Enduring the torture of withdrawal was the last thing any of them wanted. Nash looked to the next island, his words reminiscent of Tal's from the day before.

"It's not that far. We could swim it. I reckon we'd make it in twenty minutes, half hour maybe."

"It doesn't look like Tal made it," Ginger replied.

"Tal was too far gone," Nash pressed. "He was in a way worse state than the rest of us. He'd gone longer without a fix; his body and brain were wrecked. Not to mention his stupid idea of trying to swim that channel at night. Probably lost his direction in the dark, got tired, and drowned. That's how I see it."

Felix shot Nash a look of surprise. There was another likely reason why Tal hadn't made it, but neither of them had voiced that possibility yet. Nash's eyes did not meet Felix's. His next words were steeped in hunger.

"Besides, with Tal gone, there will be more junk for the rest of us."

The incentive piqued their interest. Everyone stared at the next island, judging the distance, weighing the options. Kenny didn't look so sure, but the others were becoming convinced. Withdrawal was interfering with their logic, crushing common sense more and more with every passing minute.

"If we stay we might get rescued," Kenny offered. "How 'bout we wait it out?"

"Time ain't on our side," replied Nash. "We've been here a day now, and we haven't seen shit. No boats, no planes, nothing except those fuckers on that yacht, and they're obviously not here to help."

Felix cracked his knuckles. "I ain't down with resigning ourselves to a fate when we can make our own."

Panic seeped into Kenny's voice. "Look, I really think we should stay—"

"If we stay we'll all lose our damn minds," Nash said. "And then what? We die of thirst or hunger, and rot on this island."

His opinion carried real weight now, swaying the group. Staying behind suddenly seemed like a death sentence. When Ginger spoke she seemed to speak for everyone, even Kenny.

"We should eat the rest of the food, drink all the water. We're going to need the energy for the trip."

Nash nodded. "Let's make our move in an hour."

Sixteen

"**I**f they don't move soon," the tallest man said, "we'll have to do something about it."

Four men stood on the deck of the motor yacht, the obvious leader among them giving orders. He was older than the others, early forties, and he'd been in more battles than all of them put together. Even at a distance there was something not right about his face, discolorations marring the inhuman textures that passed for skin. His blue irises were so pale that at a glance it seemed only black pupils were centered in the whites. When he grinned it looked like a hideous wound. The cruelty that festered in his mouth was the product of years immersed in savagery. The others were unaffected by it. They were hard men, trained killers and skilled survivors. Buchanan, Reposo, and Turk, the remnants of a special forces detachment, now led by one man, and one man only: the one they called Greer. When Greer spoke, all ears listened.

"I want the radio and radar monitored at all times, and all of you keep an eye on the horizons. Just in case. When these folks decide to haul ass, I want no interruptions."

Each man nodded once. Buchanan ran his fingers through his cropped blond hair and cleared his throat.

"Something on your mind, Buchanan?" Greer asked.

"Just wondering if you would like me to give our guests over there a little incentive to get the ball rolling."

Greer gave another of his unnerving grins. "Let's see if they participate of their own free will first. Then we'll see what we can do about encouraging them."

He turned his attention to the five stranded on the beach and watched their movements with disdain. Junkies, each and every one of them, the kind of parasitic lost causes Greer wouldn't think twice about shooting in the back of the head and kicking into a shallow grave. Miami was full of these wasters now, the disease of addiction and AIDS spreading through city blocks faster than an epidemic of bedbugs. The rampant crime that followed in order to fuel the fixes of these bottom-feeders angered Greer even more. His hometown had never seen such pestilence. Greer had regularly dispatched far better men in third world countries. Seeing his homeland infested

154

with such sorry excuses for human beings made his blood boil.

They're nothing but paving stones on the road to ruin, Greer thought.

Damn scabs. He encountered them almost everywhere he went, hanging on corners with teeth knocked out of their heads and a stench about them, glassy eyed and willing to do just about anything for the promise of another hit. Dope fiends desperate for a dollar had offered Greer every stolen good and sex act known to man. Courage, strength, honor, discipline—these addicts knew no such things. They were weak, good for nothing more than to be fed upon. The weak would be the sustenance of the strong. Greer feasted on the inferiority.

"One down, five to go."

"I can't believe we lost one already," Turk said. "What a waste."

"Shit happens," replied Reposo, his native New York accent unmistakable. "We can't control the chaos all the time."

"And what would be the fun in that?" Greer chuckled. "Chaos is a wonderful thing. Chaos . . ."

". . . is the score on which reality is written," the others said in unison.

They knew that score well. Innumerable situations had seen them surrounded by chaos, and on each occasion they had made the chaos their own, fighting fire with fire, burning everything to the ground. As Greer had taught them, the trick was to become the phoenix before striking the match.

"Beer, anyone?" Greer asked.

All heads nodded. Greer stepped into the cabin and grabbed four bottles from a cooler inside the doorway. He cast a glance at the loose pile of hundred-dollar bills on a card table nearby and wondered who would be the lucky winner this time out.

"We got movement on the beach, boss," Turk said.

Greer came back out, handing a beer to each of his men. He put a Cuban cigar between his lips and Buchanan leaned over with his lighter. Protruding from his mouth, it looked the opposite of every iconic image, a length of smoldering shit clasped between the teeth of some foul, vicious anomaly. Greer took a heavy drag and held it in, smiling as he watched the stranded pick at their food.

"Well, that's a good sign," he said, exhaling thick smoke. "It looks like they've finally started eating."

Seventeen

Eating was harder than anticipated. Grinding food with aching jaws and teeth was a painful prologue to swallowing mush down sore, ragged throats. Guts wanted to reject everything that entered. The stranded cupped hands over mouths as they chewed, gulping hard and fast to keep their intake from racing back up. Kenny proved least successful. Nash watched fresh vomit seep through the boy's gate of fingers again and again. Ordinarily such a sight would be nauseating, but Nash felt strangely detached as he watched the kid puke. Felix seemed to be doing the best out of them, never retching or heaving. Every time the vomit tried to come he growled it into submission.

When they had eaten all they were capable of, they washed their sickly meal down with bottled water.

Nash sat back and stretched out his stomach to aid digestion. Ginger stood and gave him an impatient look.

"Getting comfy?"

"If we try swimming too soon, we'll get cramps."

Ginger folded her arms, her look changing to one of contempt. "You do know all that stuff about waiting an hour before swimming is a load of horseshit, right?"

"No, it's not."

"Yes, it is," she pressed.

Kenny took his place beside Ginger. "I think she's right, Nash."

"Fuck, like it matters," Felix grumbled. "We barely got anything in us anyway."

Nash shrugged. "Well, maybe it would be wise to take some time and talk about what we're about to do."

"We're going swimming," said Felix with a sneer. "What's there to discuss?"

"For starters, I wanna know if we're all in this together, or is it every poor fucker for themselves out there?"

Felix gave him a look that suggested the answer was obviously the latter. It made Ginger and Maria uncomfortable. Kenny seemed terrified by it.

"Together, of course," Ginger said. "That's the only way I can see us making it."

Maria nodded. "Yes, together is good."

Felix laughed. "Speak for yourselves."

Ginger rubbed her temples, trying to hold back the venom that was seeping into her mouth, but to no avail. Poison coated her next words.

"You're fucking full of it, Felix, you know that? What if it's your dumb ass that runs into trouble out there? What if it's you that needs *our* help? What then, huh?"

Felix laughed louder. "Trust me, girl, I can take care of myself. I've been handling my shit since I was old enough to walk. It's you who should be worried, being a skinny bitch and all."

Ginger glared, teeth grinding hard enough to flex a vein in her neck that didn't go unnoticed by anyone. She pointed at Felix, finger trembling with anger.

"Listen, asshole, whatever you think you got in upper body strength, you lack double in smarts. Don't be so fucking ignorant. Take that testicle-sized brain of yours and try thinking something through just once before you—"

"Enough!"

Nash's outburst silenced them. They turned their faces away, eyes cast down like the scolded schoolkids Nash wanted them to feel like. Felix went to say something, but Nash wasn't finished.

"For fuck's sake, drop the bickering already. We're wasting time and energy here. Think we can act like the adults we are and keep our shit together?"

"You mean like you?" Ginger snarled, breathing

hard. "Throwing a temper tantrum like a fucking four-year-old?"

"Please don't fight," Maria whispered. "It will do us no good."

Ginger locked eyes with Nash. "She's right."

The looks Nash and Ginger traded with Felix were hateful, though they argued no more. A fragile truce formed without another word. They knew more infighting would tear off the masks everyone was trying to hold in place, revealing them for the volatile messes they were fast becoming. Nash felt new pain punching behind his eyes, hammering on his optic nerve. His ear canals felt hot and sore. The heroin wasn't calling to him as much as screaming for him now.

"Do you really want that smack over there, Felix?" Nash asked, wiping sweat from his brow. "You're dead set on it?"

"What you think?"

"Well, we increase our chance of getting to it if we work together. Teamwork, shit, it's grade school logic, Felix. Even you went to grade school."

"Did some community college too, motherfucker," Felix replied and made a show of cracking his knuckles.

"Then c'mon, use your damn head. You know I'm right."

"I don't know that. Y'all might just slow me down."

Nash tried to soften his voice. "Dude, we all do this

together and we're five times more likely to make that score. Safety in numbers, know what I'm saying?"

Felix tilted his head and considered. The quiet desperation in Nash's strained tone was becoming more believable. Lies seemed less likely.

"How can I trust you?"

"I give you my word."

"Your fucking word? Oh, you gotta do better than that, son."

"All I have is my word—"

"And it ain't *nearly* enough."

Nash extended his hand. "I swear on my life. If you happen to need help, however unlikely, I'm there for you. Even at my own peril. Understand where I'm coming from? I got your back if you got mine. You dig?"

Felix's head tilted the other way, eyes boring into Nash's, trying to figure out if the man was trustworthy or absolutely full of it. Felix saw nothing that concerned him. He grabbed the hand before him and shook once.

"Yeah, I can dig that."

"Fine, good," Nash said, casting a glance at the others. "We're all agreed, then?"

Ginger and Maria didn't reply. Their position was already clear. The one person who needed to speak up wasn't saying anything.

"Kenny?" Nash asked. "You cool?"

Kenny didn't reply. He only stared at his toes in the sand.

"You good to go?" Nash pressed. "This is do-or-die time, dude."

Kenny sighed. "It might very well be do-*and*-die time if I go out there."

"Hey, I thought you said you were down for this."

"I never *said* anything."

Kenny looked at Ginger then, the one who had spoken for them all before. There was accusation in his eyes. Nash could see the tension in the young man's hunched shoulders and stringy muscles, the acne on his body looking like it might pop with the pressure. Everyone waited. Everyone except for Maria. She searched the sand and picked up the sharpest stone she could find. When Kenny finally spoke his voice was barely a whisper.

"I won't do it."

They all would have stared him down for it, trying to bend the boy's will with muted suggestion, but Kenny refused to make eye contact with anyone.

"Then we're leaving you the fuck behind, kid," Nash said at length.

The words caught Kenny in the gut, forcing out a breath of shocked air. He looked again at Ginger, this time with pleading eyes, hoping she might offer to hang back. Her eyes told him she would not.

"Forget him," Felix said. "Let's get on with it."

He walked to the water's edge alongside Nash and Maria. Ginger lingered, finding it hard to turn her back on the only person in the group she had a soft spot for. Finally, she stepped to Kenny, neck strained, eyebrows knitted together cruelly. He leaned in and listened as she whispered. He grew more and more agitated with every hushed sentence she spoke before abandoning him to regroup with the others.

"Hell of a swim," Felix said, hand capped over his eyes as he gauged the distance again. "Hope we all got the nuts for it."

"Give me a knife and I'll borrow yours," said Ginger.

Nash looked back at Kenny standing on the beach. The young man's face was red and pinched. His lips were pursed hard enough to whiten.

"What the hell did you say to him?" Nash asked.

"I'd rather not repeat it," Ginger said. "Don't want to sour your opinion of me."

They all turned to regard the rigid boy. A scream was stuck in his throat. His posture suggested that he was on the verge of doing something drastic.

"How long you think he'll last out here by himself?" Felix asked.

"Oh, not long," Ginger replied. "That's why he's about to—"

"Wait!" Kenny yelled. "Fuck, wait. I'm rolling with you guys."

He ran to them like a lost child reunited with kin, the redness in his face dissipating as he rejoined the group.

"What made you change your mind?" asked Felix.

Kenny didn't reply. He stayed close, practically a shadow to Ginger, though his shifting eyes glimpsed at her with trepidation. Ginger smiled, but there was no triumph in it. Whatever her words, they had broken his will. They had been necessary.

"We should stick together out there," said Kenny, a sudden gull's cry causing him to flinch.

"Agreed," Nash replied. He eyed Felix. "We'll keep it tight."

To be out in open water alone was a terrifying thought, even for Felix despite all his bravado. Still, his response was a nonchalant "Sure, whatever."

Nash shed his shirt and stepped into the sea, the shallow water around his feet colder than he anticipated. The ocean breeze brought goose bumps from his bare flesh. As the wind passed him he felt the growing gap between his body and the others. They weren't following. Nash turned impatiently on them.

"Hey, are we doing this or what?"

They stalled, fully realizing the finality of their decision. Nash stepped out of the water and drew a line in the sand with his foot.

"Here's your starting block," he said. "Cross it and you're already in the race."

No one budged.

"You all know how things will end if we stay here."

Felix pulled off his shirt and crossed. The rest followed reluctantly. Nash led them into the water until it was thigh deep. Then he took in as much air as his sickly lungs would allow and dove headfirst into an incoming wave.

The chilled sea instantly cleared his feverish head. Under the water Nash felt his heartbeat pound, quickening as something primal protested his plan to traverse the channel. He reasoned his decision again, but it was far less convincing this time. A great beast reared its ugly head, setting its sights on him.

Sweet Christ, he thought.

The monolith came toward him, preceded by an announcement that was horrifying in its assertion. Even under the water he could hear it, feel it, threatening to flatten him. It had a volume that only the ocean could afford.

You're mine, it said.

Nash saw truth. A perspective completely alien to him granted the glimpse into his harsh reality. He could barely contain the revelation. He and the others, they were mere flecks of flesh on a blue body of unfathomable dimension. The deep would take them all, sucking skin tones and white bones into the liquid void to be crushed into nothingness.

Nash let out a submerged scream, bubbles racing past his ears. He broke the surface gasping for air.

Don't do it, he thought, shuddering. *Everyone go back. Go back now.*

He wiped salt water from his eyes and swiveled toward the others, mouth already opening to tell them of his change of heart.

"Wait," Nash started. "I'm . . . uh . . . not sure—"

Felix held up a finger. "Don't you even think of backing out now, motherfucker."

Nash flinched. The others stared at him with nothing less than hatred. All that came from Nash's mouth were murmurs, his planned words dying in his throat. It was clear on each of their faces, the anger at his cowardice. If their self-appointed leader tried to renege they might just beat the shit out of him for it.

Nash cleared his throat. "I'm not trying to back out."

He could see they were committed now, as committed as he had convinced them to be. New words, ones that would save face, formed where the others had been.

"Any trouble out there and you holler," he said. "As loud as you can, okay?"

They nodded impatiently, casting wary glances at each other. Felix waded farther and dove headfirst. He resurfaced with focus and determination, apparently not even remotely feeling the ocean's enormity the way Nash had. Ginger and Maria dove next and came up nearby, bobbing chest high in the water, shocked by the cold. Kenny resisted once more. Nash didn't mind this time. In fact, he welcomed it.

"Move it, princess," Felix said.

Kenny waded in the whole way, grimacing at the temperature of the water splashing against him. Nash heard the ocean again, whispering to him between the crashing of waves.

You're all mine now.

It was Nash's turn to stall, and it didn't go unnoticed.

"Hey, this is your plan, cowboy," Ginger said. "We're following *you.*"

Nash chewed his bottom lip, wondering if he still had a way out. To veto now would discredit him completely. With great reluctance, he decided against it.

"Then I suggest you try to keep up."

And with that he was gone, swallowed by the sea. When he popped up twenty feet away he didn't look back. He clawed the surface with windmill strokes, his companions struggling to match pace. At the outset they swam in a close-knit group, but it wasn't long before Nash pulled ahead. At first he refused to open his eyes under water, but within minutes he found himself peeking. His squinted sight revealed little. A singular blue blur expanded before him, dotted with the occasional fuzzy outline of rock or reef on the sandy bottom. The blue darkened as the shallows receded. Nash suddenly thought he might know what floating in an eternity might feel like.

A fleck of flesh on a blue planet, he thought. *That's all I am.*

The glimpses into the salty expanse burned Nash's eyes. The water grew incrementally colder with every yard he traveled through it. He could hear his companions splashing behind, sounds gradually lagging as he increased the distance. Loneliness engulfed him.

Less than a mile, less than a mile, he kept thinking. *Stay focused.*

He maintained strong strokes, despite the pain infecting his muscles. Rotator cuffs seemed to grate with sand inside his shoulders, pricked with shards of glass. Triceps felt as though they were being cut out of his arms with a dull scalpel. Legs flushed with an acidic burn threatened to give out, but the starvation for junk pulled him through the water like a fish on a hook. He could already smell the cooking spoon in his head, see the yellow-brown puddle in the utensil bubbling, its texture like grease from deep-fried chicken wings pooled on a plate. He felt the needle puncture skin and plunge relief into vein. Within seconds it would wash over his pain and wrap him in a blessed blanket, snug and numb and blissful.

"Hey!" yelled Kenny, coughing seawater. "Stick together!"

Nash treaded water, frightened by the vulnerability of his legs dangling in the liquid void below. The others lagged more than sixty feet behind. Nash waited for them to close the distance, turning his attention to the yacht. It looked much larger now with its bow pointed in their direction. Nash had little doubt it had pulled in closer to watch the show. He could see the shapes of three men on the bow more clearly. They all appeared to be holding something up to their faces.

"Cunts," Nash sneered.

He looked back the way he'd come, gauging the progress. They'd made it a third of the way already. Nash felt pretty good about the remaining distance. The aching for junk was insufferable, but it was also the fuel that ignited his muscles and sinews with rabid desire.

"Come on! Swim faster!"

Felix led the others, Ginger and Maria just behind with Kenny pulling up the rear. They chopped the water with their limbs, white wakes forming behind them, the only interruption in a vast blanket of blue. When they were twenty feet away, something new sliced through the ocean's surface and made Nash's heart skip a beat.

"Shit."

A large fin rose a foot out of the water and traveled toward them, a menacing periscope in reconnaissance fifty feet behind Kenny. It followed the group's trail for several seconds before slipping back under.

"No, no, no," Nash whispered. "This ain't happening."

Felix reached him, breathing hard. When he saw the horrified look on Nash's face his exhaustion took an immediate backseat.

"The fuck is wrong with you?" Felix asked. "You look like you just been sentenced the max or something."

Nash tried to answer, but a sudden knot tied off his throat under the Adam's apple, allowing only a choked sound to leave his lips. The others reached him, trying to catch their breath. Nash coughed hard, dislodging the knot temporarily.

"We gotta keep moving. Come on."

"Need rest," Maria gasped. "Body hurts."

Ginger nodded. "Yeah, we need a minute, Nash."

"We don't have a minute."

"What's the rush, man?" said Kenny. "The island ain't going anywhere—"

"No time to stop. We have to move *now*."

Kenny's voice rose. "Look, I need a break or else I won't be able to make it."

Nash's voice rose as well. "Kenny, we can't waste time sitting here in the water."

"Why?"

"Because—"

The knot returned, cutting him off again. Nash's pupils became shifty, betraying the situation. The others eyed him uneasily, wanting context for the fear he exuded. Felix was most concerned, for he had an idea of what might be scaring Nash.

"What the hell's got you so spooked?"

Nash flicked nervous glances between Felix and Ginger. He looked back to where he'd seen the fin. Nothing was there, but that didn't give him any relief. What was once visible was now lurking somewhere below. Nash checked the water around his body, terrified of catching a glimpse of a gliding monster.

"I s-s-saw a fin," Nash stammered. "It came up behind you guys and followed for a few seconds."

All eyes widened, every jaw slackened. Kenny and Maria whirled in the water, frantically checking around their position.

"Shark?" Kenny cried. "You're telling me you saw a *fucking shark*?"

"A *fin*," Nash shot back. "It was just a fin I saw. Honestly, I have no freaking idea if it was a shark or not."

Kenny stared Nash down, furious at the man who had persuaded them to enter the open ocean. Nash gulped, guilt adding another bulge in the knot, making it hard to breathe. Maria began to whine, trying to get something out of her pocket. She displayed the sharp rock she'd found on the beach to the others. Felix eyed it pitifully.

"Oh, yeah, like that's gonna protect us."

Maria gripped the rock tighter, but the dismay on her face could not be mistaken. She began to wail a mess of incoherent Spanish. Kenny and Felix could only swear and mutter. It was Ginger who attempted a calm voice.

"Dolphin," she said. "It could've been a dolphin you saw, or a marlin or manta ray or something. There are plenty other things in the ocean with fins besides sharks."

Nash nodded, trying to appear agreeable. He didn't buy it, though. What had risen out of the water wasn't any of the things Ginger spoke of. The fin had been too big, too pointed, too *motivated*.

"Look, I don't care if it was the spoiler on a fucking Ferrari you saw out there," Felix growled. "I don't wanna be in this water any longer than we have to be."

Eager nods all around. Nash and Felix both took

the lead, staying neck and neck as they front-crawled with newfound desperation. The others followed close behind, trying hard to keep up. Nash's eyes opened wide under the water, constantly searching for danger. Only dark blue lay below, the oceanic variant of a black hole in space. Small relief came only after every third stroke, when he turned his head out of the water to breathe, glimpsing the blue sky and white clouds above.

Keep your eyes on the prize, not down below.

But he could not. The routine threatened to drive him insane: three strenuous strokes facedown in terror, followed by a breath of hope. It took all of his strength, mental and physical, to keep moving forward. Then one sight wrecked everything. Nash turned his face into the brine and his blurred vision fixed on something new. A different color showed against the blue beneath.

You're mine too, the new color seemed to say.

Fifteen feet below, an elongated gray-green shape swam in lithesome fashion across Nash's field of vision. It was big and sleek, seemingly oblivious to the fresh meat floating on the surface. Except that it wasn't. It had detected the bioelectricity of the swimmers long before.

Jesus, look at the size of that mother, Nash thought.

The sight of it sent another glut of bubbles rushing past his ears as panicked air escaped his lungs. The new visitor cruised slowly and without menace, an apex predator with all the time in the world, its very presence portentous enough. Nash froze, floating facedown, watching the shape glide away until it faded into a fold of ocean darkness.

All mine, it seemed to call back.

Nash pulled his head out of the water to gauge the remaining distance. Halfway, he figured, if they were lucky. As he treaded water something slammed into his back. His cry of shock was reflex.

"What the hell, Nash?"

Nash spun, realizing it was Ginger and for once happy to see her. She bobbed in front of him, wiping water from her cheeks. Even as she yelled, Nash was relieved.

"Why are you stopping, fool? Keep swimming—"

Ginger fell silent. Nash's face paled, bulging eyes suddenly fixing on something behind her. She turned slowly until she saw the very thing she prayed she wouldn't. The fin had climbed out of the water again, closer this time and moving toward them with more intent. One look and Ginger knew it wasn't a dolphin, or marlin, or manta ray.

"*Shark!*" she screamed.

The others snapped their heads out of the water. One by one, they caught sight of the gray triangle heading for them. Felix let out a guttural roar, bracing for the beast's arrival, smacking the water's surface with his big, black hands. Kenny and Maria imitated him with high-pitched screams, striking the surface with no less ferocity.

"What do we do?" wailed Ginger.

Nash beat the water white around him. "Make noise. Try to scare it away."

Ginger copied, hoping to dissuade their would-be attacker. Before it reached them, the fin broke left and slipped under, implying a change of direction. The five swimmers waited breathlessly. The fin did not resurface.

"I think . . . think we scared it off," Kenny panted.

A quivering smile cracked Ginger's otherwise terrified face. "Yeah, yeah, I think you're right. I think we did."

"A shark that size ain't gonna be scared for long," roared Felix. "Let's *move*."

Felix plowed through the water, the others right behind. Nearby, the yacht slowly turned and began to cruise parallel to them. The three figures on the deck were joined by a fourth. They moved starboard side to watch the proceedings. A voice with an unmistakable Southern accent called out.

"Thought you'd like to know, they got a taste for human blood."

Laughter from the others followed. Nash swam hard, but couldn't help checking over his shoulder, looking for the fin closing in. He was so concerned with what might come up behind, he failed to see what came up on his right. In fact, none of the swimmers saw the dorsal fin of the seventeen-foot tiger shark traveling beside them before it submerged again seconds later.

"Almost there!" Felix yelled. "Only a couple hundred yards!"

New hope welled up within each of them. Nash could see the beach ahead clearly, the distance between it and him shortening with every frantic stroke and kick he delivered into the sea. He was sure they'd make it.

"C'mon, we can do this."

His newfound faith was shattered by a single scream. Nash whirled to see Kenny bobbing in the water, face pale and mortified.

"What? *What?!*" Nash demanded.

"Something *bumped* me," screeched Kenny.

"Aw, Jesus, are you bitten?"

Kenny looked down, searching for any sign of shark or blood. There was neither.

"No, I don't think so," he wailed. "Looks like I ain't been bit."

"Okay, then, keep moving. We're almost—"

Nash rocked hard in the water as something crashed into his legs below. A large, rough body scraped his shins, feeling like some kind of fuselage covered with sandpaper. The massive pectoral fin clipped his dangling feet as the tiger shark passed. He squealed and pulled up his legs, looking down in time to glimpse a monstrous tail before it flicked and disappeared. He waited to see if the water would cloud red from a fresh wound. It didn't.

"Move, move, move!" Nash screamed. *"This shark just found its balls!"*

Nash tore through the water, swimming with head up at all times, scanning the surrounding surface, picturing rows of razor teeth around a black gullet lunging for him from a nearby wave. Within a minute another scream from Kenny stopped everyone.

"I'm going back!"

Felix couldn't believe what he was hearing. "What?"

"Something bumped me again," Kenny sobbed. "Fuck this, I'm turning around."

"Don't be retarded, we're almost there."

Kenny became hysterical. "Screw you guys! This was a stupid, stupid, stupid idea. Can't believe I fucking listened to you. I'm going back!"

Nash raised his voice as much as he dared. "Don't you dare do it, Kenny, we have to stick together."

They all swam to the kid, forming a loose circle around him. Their closeness brought no comfort.

"I said I'm going back and that's final."

Before Nash could say anything more, a hand gripped his shoulder. It was Maria. She pulled, turning him so they were face-to-face. Her eyes were as cold as steel, her gravelly voice even more so.

"No, let the coward leave. The *diablo* wants him. Let the *diablo* have him."

"Fuck you, bitch!"

Kenny struck out at Maria, the back of his hand catching her hard across the cheek. Her head flew back, submerging for a second. She resurfaced, coughing seawater. When she turned her eyes on Kenny they were ablaze.

"Bastardo."

There was something in Maria's hand when she struck back. They all saw it. The sharp stone cut into Kenny's forearm as he raised it to block the attack. Everyone watched in horror as a four-inch gash opened, spilling blood into the sea. A wail rose from Kenny's throat. The stone dropped from Maria's hand into the water with a plunk.

"Maria, what have you done?" croaked Ginger.

Maria said nothing. Her eyes remained steely as she watched the blood pour. Felix lunged forward and grabbed the woman by the hair, wrenching her sideways, making her yell out in pain.

"What did you do, you crazy bitch?" Felix bellowed.

Maria pulled away with a howl, leaving a clump of black curls in his grip. Felix lunged at her again, but she was already out of reach and swimming for the island. Kenny looked to the others for help, but they kicked away from him, avoiding the growing cloud of blood in the water.

"Oh, God, I'm bleeding. I'm bleeding all over the place. Please, you gotta help me stop it. Help me stop the blood."

Nash's mouth went dry. "Sorry. I'm . . . so sorry, kid."

"Don't leave me here!"

Nash kicked farther away. Kenny began to cry. Ginger fought her survival instincts and tried to swim back to the boy.

"Ginger, don't," said Nash.

"We can't just leave him, Nash. We have to try—"

Another fin, this one smaller and with a white tip, cut the surface ten feet from Ginger and silenced her.

"We got a new guest!" Felix cried.

He flicked nervous glances between Kenny and the island, unsure of whether to stay or swim on. Nash shook his head at Ginger, warning her to forget the suicide mission she was considering.

"Kenny, you can make it to shore if you want to," Nash said. "*Swim* for it, man, before they get a fix on you. You got time."

"I can't—"

"Yes, you can."

"C'mon, sweetheart," Ginger pleaded. "Follow us to safety."

They started to swim, trying to lead Kenny along.

Nash could hear the kid sobbing behind him, but he refused to look back. Ahead, he saw the large fin of the tiger shark emerge and cut across his path before disappearing. The safety of the beach was less than a hundred yards away, Maria almost halfway to it. Nash could even make out a dark cube, the second trunk, lying on the sand. He whispered a prayer, his first in years, pleading for divine intervention.

"Please, God, we're almost there. Let us all get there in one piece."

God wasn't taking requests. Another shriek rang out before Kenny was dragged under, water garbling the rest of his cries. Nash spun in time to see one of the boy's flailing arms submerge, the tiger shark's fin sinking down on top of it. A violent thrash of tail followed, splashing the surface, then nothing.

"Kenny!" screamed Nash.

Felix and Ginger saw only ripples circling out from where Kenny went down. They waited, frantically looking for any sign of boy or shark. Suddenly, a third of Kenny's body shot out of the water, his mouth agape in a silent scream, sucking in needed air. His left arm was gone, severed below the elbow, blood ejaculating from a ragged stump and reddening the sea around him. Kenny's eyes, wide and terrified, fell on the drapes of serrated flesh hanging from what was left of his arm. Skin and sinew, muscle and bone, all washed clean, looking like something displayed in a butcher's window. Kenny's screams grew hoarse.

"Help me, for Christ's sake!"

Nash bared teeth. The sight of the kid begging in the water tore at his heart. He wanted more than anything to go back, but a rescue attempt was suicide with the sharks encircling and Kenny reduced to a piece of profusely bleeding bait. More splashing sounds came—from what, Nash didn't see—but it made the decision for him to abandon the boy for good. As he put more distance between them, Kenny's pitiful cries became enraged.

"Don't leave me, you fuck!"

Nash looked back one last time, tears in his eyes. Kenny was trying to paddle after them using his ravaged stump, splashing and dipping in the water like a panicked pup, breath coming in high-pitched wheezes. His mouth hung in an upturned crescent, whitened lips trembling. Nash could see it in the boy's eyes, the realization that his time was up.

"I'm so fucking sorry," Nash sobbed.

Kenny shut his eyes and thrashed blindly, streaming tears obsolete in the seawater. Nearby, Felix and Ginger watched helplessly, unable to bring themselves to aid the young man. Another splash nearby, a white-tipped fin glimpsed between the waves.

"Nash, we gotta go," said Felix. "Right fucking now—"

His lips trembled, unable to form more words. The tiger shark came again. The tip of its fin cut toward Kenny, quickly climbing to full height before the shark's back broke the surface. It raced for him, the sudden speed astonishing before it raised its snout above the water in a topside assault. From the side profile, Nash saw one jet-black eye roll back as a protective layer of white flesh slid over it. Jaws opened to their apex before clamping onto Kenny's shoulder, sinking multiple rows of sickle-shaped teeth into his flesh, penetrating to bone. Kenny's cry of pain barely registered as the shark's weight pushed him under. The others waited as long as they dared, hoping he would resurface again. He did not.

"Kenny?" Ginger said, searching the waves in shock. "Sweetheart?"

Loud cheers came from the yacht. Two of the figures pumped fists in the air, while the others swigged from bottles in their hands.

"We got company," Felix said, his eyes locking on something new.

Two smaller fins broke the surface in a succession of quick thrashes above the blood-clouded spot. Oceanic white-tipped sharks had arrived, drawn by their ability to smell a single drop of blood in the water from over a football field away, and they wanted in on the action. A third fin of the same species joined, but suddenly veered away, rushing through the water as the much larger tiger chased it off.

"Kenny's a goner," Nash said. "Nothing we can do for him now."

Ginger shook her head, bewildered. "We can't leave him out here, he needs us—"

Nash shook her fiercely. "Snap out of it. He's fucking fish food now and we'll be next if we stay here another second."

"But, Kenny—"

The slap he delivered across her cheek returned Ginger to her senses. They resumed their desperate swim, bloody water splashing tumultuously behind them as fins and tails lashed the surface, tiger and white-tips fighting over the fresh kill. Felix looked back and saw something pink and ripped float to the surface, where it bobbed for a few seconds before being rammed by a gray torpedo nose and taken back under.

"Swim faster!" he shouted. "It's a feeding frenzy back there!"

They clawed the water until their muscles burned, the last hundred yards threatening to break them. Hoots and jeers sounded from the nearby yacht. Nash dared not look back, dared not even open his eyes as he swam. As they neared the beach Felix stopped long enough to check the depth, his toes skimming the bottom. In another six strokes he was able to stand in four feet of water, less than thirty yards from the shore. A wide, giddy grin split his face.

"It's shallow!" he cried. "We're safe."

Ginger and Nash checked for themselves, both letting out a hysterical laugh as their feet touched down on the sandy bottom.

"We made it," Felix laughed. "We—"

Felix's grin fell away. He pointed a finger in the direction they had come. Nash and Ginger turned to see a white-tipped fin cruising toward them, the shallow water not deterring its pursuit one iota.

"Get to shore."

The group half ran, half swam toward the beach. Nash could feel the shark gaining on him with every struggling lurch he took through the shallows. Small waves pushed at his back, but didn't seem to help him forward. In three feet of water he looked over his shoulder, eyes connecting with the dorsal fin of the determined hunter, still advancing despite the decreasing depth.

"He's still coming!" Nash yelled. "Felix, watch out!"

Felix stumbled and fell into the water with a splash. Nash went to him, grabbing his arm and helping him to his feet. The extra seconds counted against them. The shark was too close.

"We've run out of road," Felix panted.

He rose to full height, water lapping against his

stomach, fists at the ready. Nash decided to keep the promise he'd made and held his position. The white-tip closed in, racing through the shallows with a sudden burst of speed, snout targeting Nash specifically. Instinctively, he grabbed for it as it lunged, palm forcing snout upward as the shark's weight pushed him back. Nash held on, staring in terror at what was in his grip. Beady eyes rolled blindly. Jaws snapped and body thrashed. Hundreds of teeth, designed to shred flesh, came within inches of Nash's face.

"Get this thing off of me!"

In an instant Felix brought a heavy fist down on the shark's right eye, clobbering it with enough force to knock it sideways. The white-tip jarred in the water and froze, momentarily stunned. Felix stepped forward and tried to land another, but the beast came to, firing itself away with a swish of its tail, its refracted image disappearing under the waves.

As soon as Nash and Felix lost sight of it they made for the beach. Ginger and Maria were already collapsed on the shore, waves washing against their legs. Maria vomited into the surf. Ginger sobbed, beating the beach with a fist, dirty matted hair strung across her face. The men dropped to their knees beside the women. Nash planted his face into the wet sand and kissed it. He turned caked lips toward Felix and forced a smile.

"Teamwork," he said, panting. "What did I tell you?"

Felix couldn't catch his breath. He gave a nod of approval, offering a thumb in the air and a pat on Nash's back.

"Teamwork," Ginger snarled. "I was just thinking about that."

Maria looked up, eyes glassy, string of saliva hanging from her chin. Ginger lunged, her full weight crashing into the smaller woman and sending her sprawling. In a flash she was straddling her, pulling hair and scratching skin.

"You made a *sacrifice* out of that poor boy, you cunt!"

Ginger's fingernails raked over Maria's cheek as she tried to gouge her eyes. Screams and Spanish filled the air. Felix pulled the women apart and hauled them to their feet. He let Ginger go, but held on to Maria.

"Here's what we're going to do, ladies," Felix started, voice rising. "We're the ones who made it. So, we're gonna open that trunk, divide up some drugs, and fucking celebrate. We're gonna enjoy our share, and Tal's share, and Kenny's share, and . . ."

He turned a wry smile on Nash and Ginger, which fast became a sneer. They barely saw the punch that Felix delivered to Maria's jaw. She dropped like a stone and hit the beach, out cold, fresh blood in her mouth. Felix watched it dribble from her open lips onto the sand.

"And we're gonna enjoy *that* bitch's share too."

A clamor of claps and cheers arose, drawing their attention out to the water. The yacht had dropped anchor a couple hundred yards from the island, the four figures on the bow applauding and waving. Nash noticed one of them holding what looked like a video camera.

"Think you were right, Ginger. We are on *Candid Camera*."

Ginger saw it too. "Sick fucks."

Felix extended his middle finger, holding it high for them to see. Laughs and boos exploded from the boat, chiding his gesture.

"Go to hell, you limp–dick bastards!" Ginger shouted.

More jeers crossed the water. Nash and Felix sank to the sand, nursing the aches in their bodies, heaving air into overworked lungs. Adrenaline quickly drained from their systems. Withdrawal symptoms filled the space. Ginger rolled Maria into a position where she wouldn't choke on her own blood. After a minute Felix staggered to his feet.

"How about we break out the party favors?"

He trudged up the beach toward the second box lying on the sand, Nash and Ginger hounding him the whole way, heroin the only thing on their minds. Felix unlatched the trunk and flipped the lid open to reveal a scene similar to the first box. He rummaged inside, pushing past the food and water until he found a small metal container. He lifted it out, shaky hands gripping it tight.

"Open it already," Ginger pressed.

They huddled together, holding their breath with pained anticipation. Felix removed the lid, exposing a baggie of fine white powder and several thin metal straws. Nash's heart sank a little at the sight. He'd expected a different modus operandi: needles, spoons, a lighter. Injecting was invariably better than snorting, but they weren't being given the choice.

"Fuck, I guess we're not cooking, then."

"They wouldn't trust us for a second with an open flame," Felix said. "No signal fires, remember?"

Nash remembered. The yacht men were adamant about covering all bases for their little game. Felix lifted the baggie out and discovered a plain white envelope underneath. He tossed it back in the box without opening it, uninterested in its contents.

"Let's get our snort on."

Felix shut the lid of the trunk and prepared the dope on the flat of it, pouring out the heroin and dividing it into three piles. There was more of the stuff than they'd anticipated, a hell of a hit for each of them. Ginger and Nash each drew a straw from the container and waited for Felix to finish. He finally raised his eyes to those of his companions, a quivering smile beckoning them closer.

The little mounds of pale dust hypnotized them. They stared, wide-eyed and grinning as they scratched at their skin.

"Dig in," Felix whispered.

They dropped to their knees around the trunk and bent over their allotted piles, straws jammed up nostrils, sucking opiate powder into nasal cavities. They felt a mule's kick the moment the drug dusted membranes.

"Oh, my God," Nash gasped.

The note on the previous island hadn't lied. The junk was the finest he'd ever consumed. Nash fell back onto the sand, feeling a cool worm twist and turn through his gray matter. The heroin's rush washed every one of his cares away. It was heaven.

Eighteen

They looked to the heavens where the first stars of emerging night glinted. Such beauty was rare, a horizon of embers shimmering on the sea, the setting sun the color of backlit blood. When dusk came to the Keys, prime feeding time came with it. The sharks would be back on the hunt soon if not already. Greer sat in a deck chair on the bow of the yacht, puffing a Cuban cigar and watching the four bodies on the beach through a pair of binoculars. The stranded had been indulging in their prize for hours now, writhing and squirming on the sand like unearthed worms, too high to care about the sunburns covering their bodies. Even Maria, recovered from Felix's punch, had been allowed to sample some leftovers from the others.

Without taking his eyes from the lens, Greer

grabbed a bottle of beer from the deck and took a swig, cigar still locked in the corner of his mouth. An amber trickle escaped his lips, dribbling past a chin of mottled skin once melted by white phosphorus. He wiped away the line of liquid with a grunt.

"Sharks aren't on the ball," he grumbled. "We should have lost two today."

Buchanan leaned against the rail beside him, picking at a plate of steak and rice, watching the beach with mild interest.

"Mr. Jones last night makes up for it," he said between mouthfuls. "I didn't realize he was so starved when we picked him up. He went downhill so fast, kinda jumped the gun."

"Ah, you never know with these maggots."

Buchanan nodded. "Still, I wish I'd seen that coming. We could have gotten great footage from it. It looked like he really got torn apart out there."

"Yeah," said Greer. "What a waste."

"Not for me."

Buchanan's smug smile annoyed Greer. Tallahassee Jones's unexpected death early in the proceedings favored the odds that Buchanan had put his money on. A correct first pick paid out an automatic thousand-dollar bonus from the pool. Greer was now tied with him in light of Kenny's demise, whom he had correctly selected as the second fatality. Neither of them had picked two for two so far, both betting that one of the women would have died in the early stages. Turk and Reposo were fishing at the stern of the yacht, the current winner and loser respectively. Reposo was zero for two, neither the heavyset Felix nor the waif-thin Ginger coming up a corpse. Turk led the group. Both his picks had turned out perfect.

"That feeding frenzy toward the end should have snagged another body," said Greer. "I can't believe they escaped that. At least *four* sharks picked up their scent, for Christ's sake."

"That was a close call in the shallows," replied Buchanan. "I tell ya, that Felix must have been one hell of a boxer back in his day."

"You would know." Greer chuckled. "I hear he got a punch over on you a few days ago."

"That was dumb luck," Buchanan replied. "And he barely grazed me."

"Sure, sure," Greer said with a smirk and looked to the beach again. "They've all got some fight in them, I'll give them that. And they're trying to stick together out there. That's . . . unusual."

Greer thought about the camaraderie that was starting to grow among the stranded. Violence and despair were bringing them together, as they had done with him and others many times before. His mind drifted. Memories came, of gunfire and explosions, of orders shouted and orders followed. Memories of men he was responsible for taken from him for all the wrong reasons. For years he'd been up to his eyeballs in drug interdiction operations, military sanctioned and CIA backed, combing the Afghan countryside for poppy crops and makeshift production facilities that in turn funded Taliban insurgents and terrorist cells. *Poisoning the wells* was how his superiors described his job. *Fucking them from behind* was how Greer viewed it. Hacking at the snake's tail was supposedly easier than trying to cut the head off, but the danger didn't diminish much. Given the opportunity, a snake's strike was swift and sure from any angle.

What a waste, Greer thought.

"Sir?"

He remembered trying to put Sergeant Sonnen's head back together, split above the eyebrow by a sniper's bullet a moment after Greer had ordered him to check a corner. He remembered the mortar round that came down on his squad a week later, shredding Specialist Wright's body apart and leaving the rest of them untouched for some reason. He remembered Specialist Craddock disappearing in an IED explosion the following day. The only part of him they'd located afterward was a combat boot, foot still inside. Greer remembered the loss of each and every man who had ever been under his command. The ones he'd risked his own neck to save he remembered even better, dragging them injured and bleeding from an ambushed convoy to safety as machine-gun fire sprayed their position. Three of them were the very men who shared the boat with him now, and each would lay down his life for him. War was indiscriminate, but Greer was not. His men were never expendable, regardless of the "big picture" that the higher ranks loved to refer to whenever discussing the loss of his highly trained soldiers on the battlefield.

What a terrible waste.

And then there was Pike, the closest thing to a brother Greer had ever known. Sergeant Major Pike, Greer's second in command since the start of the war, a career soldier who saved his captain's life on more than one occasion, an operator who after years of brutal efficiency began to have trouble coming to terms with his actions, a man who returned home after his last tour and hit the bottle hard.

Two weeks after landing back in Miami on leave, Pike found himself in a dive bar in Opa-locka, downing cheap beer until he was slurring his speech and falling off his stool. At closing he was tossed out onto the street, where he staggered back and forth until a couple of addicts found and cornered him. They demanded his wallet, watch, wedding ring, even his dog tags. Sober, Pike could have killed both of them in seconds with his bare hands, but inebriated he was no match for two opponents. Still, he tried to fight his muggers off. They dragged him into an alley and beat him to death for his efforts.

After Greer beat the bar manager within an inch of his life for the security cam footage, he'd found the pawn shop where Pike's effects had been fenced. It only took the severing of one finger before the shop owner gave up the sellers. The information led Greer to a shoddy vacant apartment strewn with drug paraphernalia. He waited, and when the junkies responsible for Pike's death returned to cook up a score, Greer took his silenced Glock and put a .45 hollow-point in each of their stomachs to ensure a slow, agonizing death. With a framing hammer, he broke both of their jaws so they could not scream for help. Then he sat and watched them for some time as they tried to crawl away, punctured guts leaving blood trails on the filthy linoleum. He watched, ignoring their incoherent moans for mercy, until their bodies stilled, knowing that he'd done something right, something just.

"Captain?"

And when a crack whore had unexpectedly hammered on the junkies' apartment door, demanding drugs and refusing to leave, Greer invited her inside and snapped her neck.

"Captain Greer?"

Greer snapped out of it. "Sorry, Sergeant, what did you say?"

"I was wondering which of our contacts you think is ready for retirement, once we get back to Miami."

"You got an opinion on that?"

Buchanan nodded. "I think that Catraz guy is wasting our time now. I'm sure we can get more out of Curtis Moffat if we put the squeeze on him."

"I agree."

Greer took a heavy drag on his cigar and peered across the channel of water he and his men affectionately called "the Killing Lanes." His eyes rested on a dark fin cutting through the shallows. It sailed parallel to the nearby beach, knowing the prey that had escaped it earlier was now just beyond reach. Soon another fin appeared. They were patrolling, waiting for another opportunity.

"Think these scabs will be as eager to continue after today?" Buchanan asked, stifling a yawn.

"Once that heroin gets its claws in them, they'll be more inclined," Greer replied. "They always deliver during the second leg."

Greer finished off his beer. His hand slipped to his hip and patted the grip of the army-issue M11 holstered there, the gun that never left his side. Greer was not an emotional man, but the smile on his face implied a kind of gleeful satisfaction. He raised his binoculars again to look over the stranded on the beach, wondering who would be the last of the lot.

"I like it when it gets down to one," he said. "Go get some rest, Sergeant. I'll take first watch of the night."

Nineteen

The night passed in a euphoric blur. With two dead from the original group, the survivors had plenty of heroin to go around. They indulged, snorting again and again, throwing their heads back to stare at the moon and stars as the opiate seeped into their bloodstreams. The worms in their heads grew fat and satisfied, rolling cool and wet through their disjointed thoughts.

For the first time they enjoyed each other's company, laughing giddily as junk coursed through their veins. They strode and staggered around the trunk, shouting, dancing. Every now and then one of them would collapse into a giggling heap. Once or twice the heroin's potency caused them to forget their ordeal completely. At all other times the horror was kept dulled and distant enough, though they instinctively avoided the water. In the darkened sea a half dozen fins patrolled the shallows, never changing speed, gliding to kill time. Had there been enough light for any of the stranded to see the lurking predators, one or two would have considered taking the easy way out. The intake of one whole pile at once might have been enough to finish someone, yet the thought of overdosing never crossed their minds. When the last of the heroin had been consumed the survivors fell into a deep, uninterrupted slumber.

But inside that slumber, worlds were turned on their heads. The dreams that came were so vivid, so effective, so rooted in alternate realities of what might have been, that it brought tears to the closed eyes of those sleeping. Felix dreamed of fighting, using his fists to save his deadbeat mother from abusive men, being the protector he'd always wanted to be and not the attacker he'd been groomed to become. Ginger dreamed of pursuit, chasing a small laughing boy around a raggedy garden until she snatched him up and held him tight. Nash dreamed of fame, playing his guitar onstage night after night to crowds of adoring fans under multicolored spotlights. Maria dreamed of home, walking the white beaches of Cayo Coco with her brothers and sisters, now grown up, pointing at crabs scuttling under shrubs while they consumed mouthfuls of dark rum and talked of a past that never happened.

Nash woke late next morning in considerable pain. His body felt drained. His joints were rusty, his stomach empty and rumbling. Every muscle in his body ached, his exposed skin sore and hot from sunburn. The others slept nearby, covered in the sand they had rolled in during the night. Nash crawled on hands and knees around the trunk, examining the lid for leftovers, wanting another taste. Not a single speck of white dust remained. He decided to address the issue of hunger, though it was a distant second. He opened the box and rummaged inside.

Food and water lay within, like the box before, but what grabbed Nash's attention was the new envelope among the supplies, the one that Felix had discarded the previous afternoon. Nash went to grab it, but stopped short, his fingers tingling, unsure of whether to even touch it. He suddenly remembered the blood, the screaming.

Don't leave me, you fuck!

Everything came rushing back, the horrors of the days before revisited in a single moment—Tal gibbering and drooling, fins slicing through sea, the bump that rocked Nash in the water like a buoy. And then the memory of Kenny came, his cries for help and shrieks of pain echoing inside Nash's head. He saw it all again, running like a film reel, the boy trying to swim to safety with a stump for an arm before being dragged under the waves by a streamlined shape with glassy black eyes and endless pointed white in its mouth.

Nash felt sick. A new nausea, brought on by fear and not chemical dependence, cramped his chin and twisted his guts. He glanced nervously at the sea. It was calmer than the day before, small waves rolling toward shore, softer sounds of them crashing on the beach. The ominous yacht was in the same spot. Only one figure sat on the deck. The figure waved to Nash. He ignored it.

"Up bright and early, I see," Nash mumbled. "You don't want to miss a damn thing, do you?"

Nash's trembling fingers plucked the envelope from the box. He inspected it, wondering if his tormentor's fingerprints were on it. They were too careful, Nash knew, too precise. He tore open the envelope and slid out the letter.

> *Dear civilians,*
>
> *Congratulations on surviving the first swim. You have now successfully completed one half of your ordeal. You will find this box identical to the last one, with the added bonus of your promised heroin. We hope you enjoy your prize. You've earned it. There is another island to the north of this one. You must traverse the channel in order to reach the third and final box. Box*

*#3 has a much larger supply of heroin and food
within it. There are further instructions to
retrieve something more for your troubles. A
small boat and navigational equipment have
been left for you on the beach, which you may
use to reach safety.*

Nash groaned. He wanted the game to be over already. Only the mention of heroin and a means of escape stopped him from losing all hope. He read the letter over again, reaffirming the few details provided. The man on the yacht stood and walked around the deck, attracting Nash's attention.

What's your deal? he thought. *Just who the hell are you—*

The tap on his shoulder caused him to scream out in surprise, a primal, pathetic sound. He threw the note up in the air, where the breeze carried it for a moment before ending up crushed in Felix's grip.

"Christ!" Nash put a hand to his heart. "Don't sneak up on a dude, dude."

"How much shit are we in?" Felix asked, looking at the paper in his grasp.

"Neck deep, if we're lucky."

Felix smoothed out the letter and read it over carefully to verify. His expression never changed. He hadn't expected anything less.

"Not out of the woods yet," he said. "I can't say I'm surprised."

"At least there is a way out of the woods," Nash replied.

Felix looked at the moored yacht. "So they say."

"You're not buying it?"

"Not buying it entirely."

He handed the letter back. Both men mulled over what they'd just read in silence, taking advantage of their newly calmed minds. The heroin in the night had set the clock back on their collective time bomb, but they knew it wouldn't last long.

"Can I see the letter?" Ginger asked.

She'd awoken and was sitting up, wiping sleep from her eyes. Maria lay nearby, curled up in a ball, eyes still closed.

"Sure, if you want to wake up on the wrong side of the bed," said Felix.

"Look around," Ginger replied, yawning, holding out a hand for the letter. "Someone totally shit the bed. It's the wrong side no matter what."

Felix didn't laugh and that was enough to snap Ginger out of her grogginess. Nash handed her the letter without a word. She stood and read it over before dropping it back in the box with a grunt.

"Hell no," she said. "I ain't going through that again."

"None of us want to," replied Nash.

"Good."

"But I don't know if we have a choice. . . ."

Ginger folded her arms. "Fuck that, Nash. I've got a choice and I'm sure as hell gonna trust my instincts over yours this time."

"Ginger, your instincts were the same as mine and you fucking well know it."

"Bullshit."

Felix nodded at the yacht. "Honey, I doubt those guys out there will be willing to give us a choice. They've given us orders, and they expect us to follow them."

"Felix," Ginger said, then paused, her resilience crumbling. "I . . . I can't do it again. You guys can go. I'll stay this time and—"

"And do what?" snapped Felix. "Wait until withdrawal kicks in a few hours from now and starts to mess you up all over again?"

"We can't stay here, Ginger," said Nash. "We'll die if we stay."

"We'll die if we *leave*," Ginger protested, pointing toward the open water. "Jesus, does anyone remember the other two guys that were with us when we started? Do we need any more proof?"

Ginger's voice stirred Maria from slumber. She raised her head from the sand, appearing to wake slowly, but her eyes were wary and ready for anything. Ginger took one look at her and the animosity between them was back.

"Go back to sleep, bitch."

Maria put her head back down, eyes like daggers flicking between Ginger and the two men. Nash noted the feral look in them. He'd seen cowering dogs act similar, ones in cages that couldn't be trusted.

"Swimming that channel was crazy in the first place," Ginger said, turning to Felix. "And to even suggest doing it again is *completely* insane."

Felix put a hand on Ginger's shoulder. "Look, I don't want to be forced to swim in desperation like we did yesterday, full of pain, feeling nothing but sick and tired. It lowers our chances."

"Our chances?" she moaned. "What chance do we really have?"

"What choice do we really have?"

"You just want more junk," Ginger said.

"And soon you will too," Felix said, looking her straight in the eye. "More and more every minute. . . ."

He was talking sense, and that irritated her. Had it been the day before, she would have surely lashed out at him. The dope consumed during the night renewed her patience. She would hear the man out.

"Furthermore," Felix continued, "I'm not sure those guys on the boat will let us quit. They didn't invest heavily in this game of theirs for nothing. We're here to partake."

Ginger snorted. "All the more reason not to give them the satisfaction then."

Felix sighed. "To be honest, I think they'll kill us outright if we don't comply."

Nash looked at the man on the deck of the yacht and gulped. He had no doubt that Felix was speaking the truth. Another man emerged from the yacht's cabin, followed by a third and fourth.

"Look, here's the deal," Nash said. "We know our kick last night was just enough to get us through the day, and then we'll be back to pain and puke. That's our vicious cycle, our lot, and right now we got a little downtime, but soon we'll need what's in that third box. And in case you haven't noticed, this island ain't the one we can escape from."

"You really think they've left a boat over there for us?" Ginger asked.

Nash shrugged. "They haven't lied about anything so far."

"I'd rather go now," Felix said. "While we feel up to the task and know what we're up against. Let's use what little edge we have to our advantage."

"You're fucking nuts," Ginger said.

Felix tried on a grin. "I hoped you wouldn't notice."

He knelt in front of the open trunk and rummaged

inside, pulling out supplies and laying them on the sand. Sandwiches, apples, energy bars, same as before. He scrutinized the sustenance before him, wishing more nutritional value had been provided.

"Little more than a snack, but it'll have to do," he said. "Y'all get stuck in now and build up your strength to swim."

"It would be good if we go close to noon," Ginger offered, checking the sun's position in the sky. "I think sharks are more active at sunrise and sunset."

"Got a feeling you're right about that dusk and dawn shit," Felix said, tossing apples to her and Nash. "I'm down for whatever stacks the odds in our favor."

Maria rose from where she lay, licking her lips, taking a few timid steps toward the food that lay before Felix. He stopped her with a glare.

"Don't think so," he said. "You can wait and see if we leave you any scraps."

She crouched. If looks could kill, the one Maria gave Felix would have drawn and quartered him.

Twenty

Kenny Colbert had indeed been torn to pieces, and much more than a four count. Not all of the kid found its way to the bellies of beasts or the bottom of the sea either. Buchanan took a net and fished some of the young man's remains out of the water near the yacht's stern. He dumped them into a bucket and examined them: a partial upper thigh, a shoulder and armpit, and a section of torn flesh with a patch of hair. Turk strolled by and stopped to have a look.

"What's that?" he asked, pointing to the unidentifiable remain.

"Nape of his neck, I think," Buchanan replied. "See the darker hair?"

"Yeah, I see it. Jeez, greedy bastards, ain't they?"

"Those white-tips are worse than jackals. I'm surprised they left this much."

Turk chuckled. "I'll bet that tiger probably had a whole half of the kid to itself."

Buchanan dumped the bucket's contents into another bucket and fastened a lid on it. Turk headed back to the bow of the boat. Buchanan followed. They stopped before Greer, who sat in his deck chair, smoking and drinking in turn.

"What was left?" he asked.

"Hardly anything," Buchanan replied. "Looks like an armpit got spat out again, though."

"What is it with all the uneaten armpits?"

Turk laughed. "Sharks must not like the smell."

"I'm not surprised," said Buchanan. "This is probably the first bath these junkies have had in weeks."

Reposo came out of the cabin with a pair of binoculars. He scanned the survivors on the beach, wondering who the weakest link was and how much it would factor into his betting strategy.

"Who do you think is next?" he asked.

"It has to be one of the women," Greer said. "I can't believe they're both still in the game at this point."

"Anyone got money on one of the girls getting bagged next?" Buchanan asked.

"We do," Turk and Reposo replied in unison.

"Redhead or Cuban?"

Reposo adjusted his binoculars, focusing on Maria sitting by herself. "My money is on the Cuban. She's ostracized herself now, and that sucker punch she took might have weakened her chances. Personally, I think she's suffering a broken jaw. That girl is damaged goods."

Greer gave a grunt. "They're all damaged goods."

Greer thought about damage. The damage he and his men had inflicted over the years, and the damage they had taken in return. He allowed it to prey on his mind for the first time in a long while, the injuries to body and soul that could never heal.

At what point are people beyond repair? he thought.

Unspeakable things came to mind. Acts committed by him and those under his command in the fog of war, both sanctioned and off the record, most of it during their tours in Afghanistan. How he loathed that fucking place, the leading producer of heroin in the world, a damned desert that was good for nothing except growing poppies and producing insurgents. No matter how many fields they razed, no matter how many drug lords or tribal chiefs they assassinated, no matter how many production houses they located and leveled with air strikes, it never seemed to put a dent in America's appetite for the drug or the Afghan's ability to supply it. Greer hated that part of the world more than anywhere else, yet he still maintained contacts there that could provide him with the finest opiate at competitive prices.

I can't fix things with my hands tied.

If he'd been allowed to fight the war the way he wanted, they would have been one step closer to winning the damn thing. During many a mission debriefing, his detractors had accused him of allowing too much collateral damage, referring to some of his actions as atrocities. Even the term *war crime* had come up once or twice, but Greer never believed that. What Greer and his men had done to the enemy outside of mission parameters was warranted, regardless of whether those behind desks back in Washington deemed it uncivilized. Their interpretation of orders eventually led to their dismissal from the ranks, and Greer had felt it unjust. He had never felt pity or remorse over what he had done. For him all was fair in love and war. Being relieved of command didn't mean the mission was over. Not for him. Not for any of them.

"You okay, Cap?" asked Buchanan.

"I'm fine."

"Something on your mind?"

"Dishonorable discharge."

Greer said no more. He threw his cigar overboard and retreated to the cabin. The others knew better than to follow him. They kept watch while Greer sat inside and stewed in his thoughts.

Twenty-One

Felix was lost in thought as he sat and watched the men on the boat. Ginger and Nash huddled together, waiting and worrying with full stomachs and frayed nerves. Maria stayed well away from everyone, unwelcome and unhappy. She hadn't said one word to them since awakening, though they'd eventually allowed her to eat what food they couldn't finish. Felix cupped a hand over his eyes and gauged the distance to the next island, wondering where the sharks were more likely to lurk.

"What are you thinking?" Nash asked.

Felix cast a glance at Maria. "You don't want to know."

"Think we'll make it?"

"We'll make it."

Ginger grunted. "And if we don't?"

Felix raised an eyebrow. "Any regrets?"

"Oh, plenty."

"Yeah? What was your biggest?"

The question seemed to punch Ginger in the gut. Her demeanor soured more. She didn't reply. Felix turned to her and cocked his head.

"Care to share, honey?"

"Maybe some other time."

"All we got is time right now."

Ginger's lip quivered. She allowed her hair to fall in her face so her companions would not see the tears that were welling up. Felix felt bad, knowing he'd scratched the surface of something, but a confession seemed timely. He breathed deep, taking in the oxygen needed to lift a certain weight off his chest.

"I killed a guy once," he confessed. "That is my biggest regret."

Ginger looked up, brushing her hair away to reveal tear tracks running down each cheek. Her face was a strange mix of relief and anguish.

"Tell me about it," she said. "Please."

Felix sighed and drew circles in the sand with a finger, letting his dreadlocks hang to hide his face. Nash and Ginger stared at him, but he wouldn't look at either of them.

"Wasn't completely my fault," he said, voice strained.

"I was young and stupid. Twenty-two years old and out to do some damage."

"What happened?" Nash asked.

Felix didn't speak for a while. He simply sat and mulled over the worst memory in his collection, motionless except for the breeze that swayed his matted hair. Just when Nash thought he might have turned to stone, the man's lips began moving.

"I was twenty-two years old," he repeated. "Twenty-fucking-two with a knack for fighting that I'd built up from a bad childhood and even worse adolescence. I had too much to be angry about, and what did they go and do? They put me in a goddamn boxing ring and told me to take out all my rage on the guy in the opposite corner."

"You killed a guy in the ring?"

The flinch was slight, but Nash saw it. The words bit Felix, just as they had gnawed at him every single day of his life since the fateful one.

"I beat Tommy 'the Sweeney' Todd to death in a clusterfuck of a fight," Felix said. "Some Limey bastard, tough as nails with a cocky mouth and a great right hook. He came over for an exhibition match and I sent him home in a body bag."

Nash and Ginger gawked at Felix, mouths unable to respond, minds processing the revelation. Felix peeked at them through his dangling hair, then closed his eyes and hung his head even lower.

"It happened in the eighth round. Tommy had gone toe-to-toe with me every second of the fight, but I'd landed a couple of stunners in the fourth and sixth and dropped him to the canvas. That damn Englishman beat the count every time."

"All fighters step into the ring knowing the risks," Nash said. "Fatalities are a reality of the sport."

"This one is on me, though. Tommy could have survived it if I hadn't kept putting him in his place. Stubborn fucker just wouldn't stay down and the damn ref kept letting him get to his feet."

Felix's hands balled into fists and shook as his voice rose. Ginger and Nash scooted back, frightened by the man's volatility.

"If he'd just stayed the fuck down, all that would've been hurt was his pride."

"Wasn't your fault," Nash said. "The fight should have been stopped."

"But it was my fault," Felix corrected. "I beat him until he didn't know where he was anymore. I beat him until the light in his eyes began to go out. Then I beat him some more. I was beating the poor fucker to death and I knew exactly what I was doing the whole time."

Nash said nothing. Ginger tried to say something comforting, but the words caught in her throat. She mumbled a sentence, none of it coherent.

"I hit the bottle hard after that," Felix continued.

"When that failed to numb me anymore, I graduated to prescription pills and then smack in order to dull my demons."

"I abandoned my son," Ginger blurted out, fresh tears coming. "I gave him up for adoption. I let someone take him away from me."

She dropped her face into her hands and began to sob. The men exchanged glances, unsure of what to say or do. Even Maria looked up from where she sat, edge of her mouth curling with satisfaction at the other woman's despair. Nash tried to put an arm around Ginger. It was instantly shrugged off.

"Your son?" asked Felix, voice uncharacteristically soft. "What was his name?"

"Justin," she said. "I named him Justin."

"And why did you have to let him go?"

"I was only eighteen," Ginger moaned, drying her tears. "Eighteen and too young and stupid to know what to do with a baby. More than anything I was too fucking selfish to even care. He was such a healthy, happy child. The kind anyone else would think was a blessing, but not me. Oh, no, Ginger had her own life to live, and it wasn't going to be tied down by the gift of some beautiful baby boy—"

Her throat bucked and she lost her words again. The stone in her chest that had replaced her heart years before was cracked through and through. The confession ground pieces of it into dust, which thickened with her blood into clay. That clay could patch her heart if only she would allow it. If only she could see her son one more time, hold him in her arms for just a moment and whisper to him how sorry she was, then maybe she could find some respite. That was what she wanted, more than heroin, more than anything: just another minute with her son.

She would speak no more of her biggest regret to the others. In the ensuing silence Nash knew it was his turn. He swallowed hard and spoke quietly.

"I took this girl home after a gig once . . . sweet little thing had been giving me the shy eye from the side of the stage all night, and I thought I'd capitalize on it."

Felix chuckled. "That doesn't sound too bad."

"Turned out she was fifteen years old."

Ginger gave Nash a horrified look and he matched it. He held out his hands to her in apology, guilt quickening his heart.

"I had absolutely no idea," he said. "She didn't look that young. She was in a club late at night with a drink in her hand. I thought she'd been carded at the door, figured she was legal."

Ginger shook her head. "So you took an underage girl home to your bed?"

Nash sighed. "I did more than that. I introduced her to heroin. Gave the poor girl her first taste that night and sent her on her way next morning."

Felix chewed that over. "And how did that work out for her?"

Nash's voice was barely a whisper. "She died."

"Overdose?"

Nash nodded. "About a year later, in some dive motel off the interstate where she'd been turning tricks for money and dope. Someone shot her up and left her alone in a room. Body was there for days before anyone found it."

He spoke no more, heart twisting in his chest the same as the others. They were beyond fucked up, emotionally wrecked and chemically imbalanced to the point where they were toxic to the hearts and souls of others they came in contact with. Their personal demons had come to roost with the skeletons in their closets, resulting in a rape that produced a broken bastard love-child in each of them. This love-child, born of heroin and regret, needed constant feeding. Sacrifice was the only thing it would eat.

They looked over their shoulders at Maria, wondering what her story was. There was something much darker about her, as if regrets weren't part of her makeup. The way she had pulled the sharp stone on Kenny and slashed at him without a second thought—it unnerved them all, even Felix. There were certainly skeletons in her closet, and they figured she'd dumped each and every one of them in there.

An idea came to Felix. He gathered himself up and

marched into the wooded area in the middle of the island. Ginger and Nash watched with mild interest as he poked around the trees and bushes. He returned a few minutes later with three short, thick sticks and a flat rock.

"What are you doing?" Ginger asked.

"Improvising."

He took one of the sticks and rubbed its tip vigorously against the rock face at an angle. Soon a point began to form.

"I'm not going back in that water without a weapon."

"Those are pretty big fish you're looking to skewer," Ginger said with a smirk. "It'll be like sticking a thumbtack in them."

"Better than nothing," Nash said. "You saw Felix coldcock that shark near the shore. They don't like being attacked any more than we do."

"Not going down without a fight," Felix said, grinning hellishly. "And if we make them bleed instead of us . . ."

Ginger's smirk dropped and she nodded. Felix sharpened the end of the first stick to a fine point and handed it to Nash, then set to work on the remaining two. With the makeshift dagger's tip Nash wrote the word *fuck* over and over in the sand beside him.

"Not going down without a fight. . . ."

Twenty-Two

"**T**hey've definitely got some fight in them," said Greer. "I'm starting to like these scabs."

Greer and Turk stood on the bow of the yacht, watching the survivors closely with their binoculars, wondering if the next leg of the game might require some motivation. Seeing three out of four moving toward the water with stick daggers in hand gave Greer hope.

"Hey, boys, come take a look."

Buchanan and Reposo appeared in the cabin doorway and stepped out onto the deck, each holding a beer. In Buchanan's other hand was his camcorder.

"Let me see," said Reposo.

Greer handed him the binoculars. Buchanan put down his camera and beer and climbed up into the cockpit of the boat to retrieve something, returning moments later carrying a .50-caliber Barrett M107. He shouldered the sniper rifle and raised the barrel. Defined biceps locked it into place, supporting the weight easily. He used its powerful scope to survey the situation.

"Why is the spic chick staying away from the others?" he asked.

"She's been avoiding them since the black one knocked her out," Turk replied. "There's some serious animosity going on. I think they might do her more harm if she gets too close."

Turk watched as Maria suddenly began walking toward the other three. There was rigidity in her posture and anger in her stride. Reposo took note.

"Hey, I think there might be another scuffle coming. Shit, do we want any of them bleeding before they get back in the water?"

"No," said Greer. "Not yet."

"Gotta keep them apart, then," Buchanan said and chambered a round in the M107. "Want me to fire off a warning shot, boss?"

Greer took a swig of beer and considered it. "Hold off for now, but keep them targeted. If anyone takes a swing, then yeah, give them a scare."

Buchanan fixed the crosshairs on Felix's torso, watching and waiting for any sign of violence. He noticed the sharpened stick in Felix's hand.

"Damn, look at those pokers," he said with a smirk. "They're starting to get innovative, aren't they?"

"Getting a little smarter too," Reposo mused, checking the sun's position overhead. "Good time to try and swim for the next island. There's a lot less shark activity this hour. I wonder if they know what they're doing."

Greer grinned. "I wonder what they're saying right now."

The four men watched as Maria began arguing with the others. Greer sat down in his deck chair, placing a pair of aviator sunglasses over his eyes. He polished off his beer before firing up a fresh cigar.

"Raise anchor," Greer ordered, puffing thick smoke. "Let's pull around and get a better view. This is going to get interesting."

Twenty-Three

"**T**his might get ugly," Ginger whispered to Nash.

Maria stood defiantly before Felix, close enough to be struck again, spittle on her weathered lips and traces of blood on her bared teeth. Ginger couldn't believe the girl had the balls to get in Felix's face after what he'd done to her the day before.

"Why you not make sharp stick for me?" accused Maria.

"You won't need one," Felix growled.

"I am to swim without?"

"Not exactly."

Maria looked at Felix's newly forged weapon, its crude tip telling her all she needed to know. She took a step back as horrible thoughts entered her mind.

"You . . . you are planning to stab me."

"What?"

"With that." She pointed. "You will stab me out there. Make me bleed in the water so sharks will come."

Felix threw his head back and laughed. "You mean, like you did to Kenny?"

Maria didn't answer. The wooden point had her attention fixed. She wished she still had the sharp stone that had been lost at sea. Felix tucked the dagger into his waistband and wagged a finger at her.

"No, I won't stab you," said Felix. "Despite what you may think, I ain't like you."

"Then why I no have?"

"Like I said before, you won't need one," Felix said, shaking his head. "Because you're staying here."

"*¿Qué?*"

"You're not coming with us, honey. And if you try to, I *will* cut you up out there and spill that bad blood of yours for the sharks."

Maria hitched in a breath of shocked air. Ginger and Nash said nothing, though they too were caught off guard by Felix's decision.

"But I will die if I stay!" Maria protested.

Maria went to step even closer, but a subtle shake from Nash's head stopped her. They exchanged a look between them, one which spoke volumes. They both knew Felix was as good as his word. If the man said he

226

would cut her, he would cut her deep. Felix walked away and waded into the shallows.

"You'll die quicker if you try to follow me," he said over his shoulder. "I can guarantee that much."

Ginger and Nash hesitated at the water's edge, pointed sticks tucked in their waistbands as if they were players in some cheap pirate pantomime. If their situation hadn't been so dire, they would have looked comical.

"We're just going to leave her behind?" Ginger asked.

Felix was resolute. "We're just going to leave her behind."

"We can't do that."

"Yes, we can. She's earned her abandonment."

Nash waded through the water toward Felix, noticing that the yacht was in motion, closer than ever. Three men were on deck, watching and waiting. The fourth stood in the cockpit, piloting the vessel. Nash got the unshakable feeling they were about to do something drastic. He put a hand gently on Felix's shoulder and whispered in his ear.

"Felix, what's going on?"

"An experiment."

"An experiment for what?"

Felix held a finger to his lips. "Wait and see."

He beckoned for Ginger to join them in the water.

She went reluctantly, casting a worried glance at Maria. Again, Maria tried to take a step in their direction. Felix wagged another finger at her.

"Don't even think about it. Stay right where you are."

Maria stayed, fixed in her spot with both fear and frustration. Nash looked upon her with pity and saw what he'd missed before. In her own way the young woman loved life. She was a survivor, one who beat the odds, clawing ahead constantly to keep from slipping back. Failing to go with them defied every instinct she had. Maria began to yell at the others, voice panicked and enraged at once. They backed away, moving deeper and deeper into the water, leaving the woman on the beach to a different fate.

∘ ∘ ∘

"Something's up, fellas," Buchanan said, squinting behind the scope of the M107. "Take a look."

Greer signaled to Turk in the boat's cockpit. Turk eased up on the throttle and slowed the boat down as Greer and Reposo raised their binoculars.

"Well, well, what do we have here?" Greer said, focusing on Maria.

Maria stood fast on the beach, face red and neck strained, her mouth a flapping hole as she shouted at the three others wading out to sea.

"What on earth is she yelling about?"

"Not sure," replied Reposo. "It's all in Spanish and I can't hear it too well."

"Looks to me like she's refusing to participate," Buchanan said. "She ain't budging from the beach. I think she's decided not to go with them."

Greer's cruel smile returned. "Is that so?"

He raised a closed fist and Turk slowed the boat to a full stop. Then he turned to Buchanan and nodded. Buchanan folded out the M107's bipod and lay down on the deck.

o o o

When the water was chest high, Felix, Nash, and Ginger began swimming. Fifty yards out Maria's angry shouts behind them became broken by the wind and waves, but the woman still spat every ounce of venom she had their way.

"Hijo de puta! Me cago en tu madre—"

The retort of the M107 echoed across the water a split second after the .50-caliber bullet struck Maria center mass.

"Jesus—"

Nash stopped swimming and looked back. He thought he saw Maria lying on the beach, but was sure he was mistaken. He wiped salt water from his eyes and looked again. It couldn't be her. What was on the beach was in two separate pieces.

"Felix!"

Felix and Ginger were already watching. The M107's .50-caliber antimaterial round, capable of putting a hole in an armored vehicle, had ripped Maria's body clean in half. Her top portion continued living for almost a half minute, eyes opening and closing, mouth moving, still trying to spew the last of the profanity her brain had formed into speech.

"We have to go back," said Nash.

Felix stared with a trembling jaw at the two halves of the woman on the sand. He'd thought a warning shot might have been in the cards, something to motivate her into the water. Not this.

"Felix?"

"F-f-forget it," Felix stammered. "She's dead. They took her out."

"They did? Why?"

Felix gulped. "Because they thought she was refusing to participate."

Nash turned on him. "That was your goddamn experiment?"

"We had to know what would happen if we didn't follow their instructions—"

"Fuck me, Felix. You're as bad as they are."

"Me? You saw what that callous bitch did to Kenny. She would have done that to any one of us this time if we gave her half the chance."

Nash figured he was right, but wasn't going to give Felix the satisfaction. He turned to swim back, wanting to get a closer look, to see if Maria really was dead. Ginger's trembling voice stopped him before he started.

"I need you, Nash."

They were the last words he ever expected to hear from her. The desperation in her tone forced him to turn back and face her.

"Don't go," she pleaded. "I can't do this alone."

"Do what alone?"

"Abandon another person like we just did."

Nash looked into her eyes and saw more fear there than he'd seen since waking up beside her two days before. It was the idea of being left behind that terrified her most, more than hungry sharks, psychotic men, or the ocean itself. Left to the mercy of such things meant you'd been abandoned. It was out of your hands, and that was the most awful part. Someone else made the decision to forsake you, leave you behind, alone and out of your element to deal with monsters in theirs.

"I won't leave you," Nash said. "I promise, Ginger."

"Hell, nobody gets left back," said Felix. "The three of us are . . ."

His mouth gaped as he watched the yacht slowly propel itself into view behind Nash's head. The buzz of an outboard engine came to their ears. Seconds later a Zodiac pulled away from the yacht's stern with a full-throttled whine, two men riding it. It seemed to be headed straight for the beach, though Felix wondered if it would veer around and head for them instead.

"Watch these guys," he said. "Don't take your eyes off them."

The Zodiac pulled into the shallows and beached itself. Both men jumped out and hit the sand, Heckler & Koch MP5 submachine guns slung over their shoulders. Nash finally got a good look at them, focusing on the one with the cropped blond hair.

"That's one of the guys that tailed me in Opa-locka, I'm sure of it."

Felix peered, straining his neck. "Yeah, looks like the redneck who winded me outside my apartment door."

The men made their way to Maria's two halves and stood over them. They talked briefly, prodding at her corpse with their combat boots. Then one of the men dragged her lower half by the legs back to the boat. The other man followed, dragging her top half by her curly black hair.

"What are they doing?" Ginger asked.

"Cleaning up evidence," Felix replied.

The Zodiac pulled away from the beach, but did not return to the stern of the yacht. Instead, it sped into the open water and slowed to a stop, where it waited, the heads of both men turned in the direction of the survivors.

"Now what?" Ginger moaned.

"We swim for the next island as fast as we can," Felix said. "And we don't stop."

They kept their heads above water this time, staying alert for any threat. Nash looked to the sky, taking in the beauty of the blue expanse crested with clouds, trying to distract himself from the darker blue that dominated below. His eyes slid over to Ginger and Felix, who to his surprise had overtaken him. The last thing Nash wanted to do was take up the rear. That hadn't worked out so well for Kenny.

Forget about outrunning the sharks, he thought, cowardice blooming inside him. *All you have to do is make sure you outrun these two.*

Nash swam hard to catch up. He had never been so scared in all his squandered life. Now and then he dared to squint into the water below, but saw only a blur of unbroken blue. Every tenth stroke or so, Nash reached down to check that the dagger was still with him. The pointed stick tucked in his waistband provided little comfort. He had checked over a dozen times when Ginger's pained voice suddenly rang out.

"Help!"

Nash and Felix wasted no time swimming to her side, ignoring as best they could the possible causes for her distress.

"What's wrong?" Nash said, reaching her first.

"Leg cramp," she squealed. "I can't get it to go."

"How bad?" Felix asked.

"Real fucking bad, all seized up. My leg is like a damn block of wood."

"Don't freak out," Nash said. "Here, I'm going to lift my calf sideways. Put your arms around my neck and stomp your foot down on it as hard as you need until you work that cramp out."

Ginger's quivering mouth tried to smile for Nash. He was there for her, coming to her rescue, a rescue that deep down she had wanted since the beginning of the whole fucked-up ordeal. She slung her arms around his neck and pulled him close in the water for just a moment, pressing her slender body against his, feeling the warmth of his skin. In that moment she knew they could have been lovers in another time, another place. In another set of circumstances she might have met him one night after a gig at the Barracuda Room and let him buy her that drink that would lead to other things.

Ginger planted a kiss on Nash's cheek, catching him off guard. Then she beat her foot down on his calf, jarring her cramp into submission. The force bobbed them below the surface of the water. When they came back up she was smiling.

"It's all gone," she gushed. "Thank you."

Nash nodded, still feeling the touch of her lips on his cheek. "Good. You okay to continue on?"

His concern was genuine, the unexpected kiss softening something in him. It was the first sliver of sincere affection he had received from anyone in a long while, and he was thankful. For him, it couldn't have come at a better time.

"I'm good to go," Ginger said and released him from her embrace.

Nash let her lead, suddenly willing to take up the rear to protect her. They swam four hundred yards, almost halfway to the next island, with no sign of the tiger shark or scavenging white-tips. Adrenaline pumped their muscles harder and faster than they had ever been tested, yet minutes seemed like hours. Nash's heart raced. His lungs begged for a break. Searing pain shot through his sinews, daring his body to give out. Even as it worsened, it was still more bearable than the withdrawal that had ravaged him on the last crossing. When they had completed two-thirds of the distance Felix called out for a breather. The three formed a huddle in the water.

"Look," he said, pointing and panting. "They're coming closer again."

The Zodiac was less than a hundred yards to their left, moving slow, matching speed as it traveled parallel to them. The two men were crouched, one of them holding up what looked like a video camera.

"The sick bastards are just waiting for a show," Nash said. "But I get the feeling they might not get one today—"

The Zodiac's idling engine roared to life and it sped up on its trajectory, curving a hundred and fifty yards ahead to where it could stop directly between the swimmers and the next island. Felix strained his neck and peeled his eyes to try to get a better look.

"What the hell are they doing?"

The man in front was hurling stuff over the side of the boat with a small container, as if bailing water out of the hull. Felix could see that what was being chucked over the side was red.

"Oh, you fucking *cocksuckers*."

"What?" Ginger moaned.

"They're chumming the water, throwing blood and fish bits ahead of us to attract the sharks into our path."

Nash gave a loud, sickly cough. "Oh, God, they're doing more than that. Look."

They watched as the man tossed both halves of Maria overboard, spilled intestines trailing over the side. Two large splashes and a single laugh sounded over the water. They could see the pieces of the woman floating on the waves.

"We should go back," Nash said, holding back the urge to vomit.

"We *have* to go back," Ginger insisted.

"That's what they want us to do," Felix replied. "When the sharks arrive they'll have more time to lock onto us if we try and return. Fuck, we're three-quarters of the way already, and I'm almost out of juice. I say we go forward."

Ginger couldn't believe her ears. "You expect us to swim through blood and *body parts*?"

"We'll give the chum a wide berth," said Felix. "Swim around it, head for the far side of the island. The sharks will be too attracted to the blood to give a shit about us for a little while."

Ginger shook her head. "Either that or the chum appetizer will get them in the mood for a main course."

The blond man dumped the rest of the bucket over the side, bits of Kenny mixed with blood and tuna spreading out over the water. The three survivors resumed their swim using breaststroke, heads above the water to monitor the situation, altering their route to avoid the chum. The Zodiac pulled away to a safe distance and waited. Soon Felix stopped, motioning for the other two to do the same. The first white-tipped fins broke the surface of the red water ahead of them.

"This is crazy," Nash panted. "So unbelievably ridiculously fucking crazy—"

"Hey," Felix snapped. "Save your energy."

A muffled whine suddenly escaped Ginger's throat, drawing the men's attention. Her hand was clasped over her mouth, eyes bulging at something behind. They turned, both stifling a cry at the sight. Forty yards away the large fin of the tiger shark rode the waves, picking up speed on approach. Nash and Felix instinctively grabbed their daggers and held them under the water to fend off an attack. As it neared, Nash noticed that the fin wasn't quite aimed at them. It was offset a few degrees, targeting something else.

"Try not to move much," he whispered. "I don't think it's coming for us."

The man-eater closed the distance quickly, drifting to their left. The three treaded water with minimal movement, noses just above the surface, watching the tiger shark cruise by less than five yards from their floating bodies. It ignored them completely, focusing strictly on the scent ahead, dwarfing them as it passed. The dorsal fin cut the water, sending ripples against their bobbing heads, the true power and capability of the creature becoming apparent to them all. Nash could see the faded stripes along its body below the surface, markings that gave the beast its name. That the creature had been bestowed with the names of two predators played on his mind. Such a title spoke volumes of its savagery.

And it's looking for lunch, Nash thought.

He felt the powerful tail push a current over his submerged body. The fin sped toward the blood and chum, diving just before reaching it. Felix let out a long shudder, his words escaping with a slow exhale of air.

"I think I just pissed myself."

"I think we all did," whispered Ginger.

They tucked their daggers away and continued on, trying to make as little disturbance as possible, beginning their wide berth of the blood and chum, noting every fin and tail that splashed and thrashed the surface. Both sections of Maria's body bobbed in the water, shrinking as bits of her were eaten away.

Targeting the far end of the island added more than fifty yards to the swim, but the enticing safety of the beach caused their quiet advance to lapse. Felix was first, splashing more as he tried to pick up the pace. Ginger followed, churning the water frothy with her limbs. Nash winced at the commotion.

"Hey, stop, you guys."

Neither of them stopped. In fact, they seemed to make more noise in light of his warning. The sharks would sense the distress soon, if they had not already. Nash shouted as loud as he dared.

"Hey! Quit making so much . . ."

He looked over his shoulder, the rest of his sentence falling down his throat and into the pit of his stomach. Maria's remains were gone. Halfway between him and the chum was a white-tipped fin, moving curiously toward the sounds of splashing, ignoring the blood behind it. The shark was one of the last to turn up, missing out on the meal of Maria. It had gulped a few pathetic scraps in the water, but was growing disinterested in the lack of actual food in the blood cloud. Nash had no doubt this shark was coming straight for them.

"Guys, stop!"

Felix and Ginger finally heard. They looked back and saw the fin. Panic gripped Ginger and she resumed swimming, splashing louder than before.

"Wait! Don't move, it will attract—"

Nash's words fell on waterlogged ears. He looked to Felix and saw the man staring back, mouth hung slack with horror. Another fin, the pointed sail of the tiger, had broken the surface behind the first fin and was coming around in their direction.

"Fuck it!" shouted Felix. "Go, go, *go*!"

They pulled hard for land, heads down, taking breaths only when necessary, closing the distance. The incoming sharks closed their distance too. Three fins now followed, two white-tips and the tiger's, gathering speed at the sound of thrashing in the water. Nash begged into the brine, promising himself that if he ever got back to the mainland, if he ever made it out alive, he would turn his damned life around, ask forgiveness from everyone he'd wronged, make amends to all that he'd hurt. All those loved ones that heroin had replaced, they'd be getting a phone call to say Nash was alive and well and wanted to see them again. He'd go to rehab. He'd go to church even. He'd be a new man, a good man, a changed man.

"We're almost there!" cried Felix.

The tiger surged ahead, leading the others like an alpha in a pack of wolves. Felix and Nash found new strength and overtook Ginger. For every yard they gained, the sharks gained three. Nash looked down into the water. He could see the bottom fifteen feet below. Seconds later an escarpment of sand sprang up, cutting the depth to five feet even though they were still a considerable ways from shore.

Nash called to the others, "It's starting to get shallow!"

Forty yards from the beach Nash stopped and stood in four feet of water. He whirled around in time to see the fins slip under one by one. Felix appeared at his right and both men braced for the sharks' arrival. Ginger lagged behind, swimming in a breathless frenzy.

"Come on, Ginger!" Nash shouted *"Come on!"*

The dorsal fin of the tiger shot up a body length behind her, lunging forward with marauding purpose. Ginger reached out and the men caught her by the wrists. They tried to pull her forward, watching the distorted image of the shark's mouth open under water, a gaping black hole surrounded by sharp white.

"Save me—"

Seawater filled Ginger's mouth. Crushing jaws closed over her left foot as Nash and Felix tried to wrench her out of reach. Her body went rigid with the bite, her gargled screams loud enough to make both men's ears ring. The shark shook her violently, teeth tearing through ligaments and tendons, sawing down to her tibia, where they snapped the bone like a pencil. Nash watched it swallow her foot in one gluttonous gulp before pulling away.

"Oh, God . . . Ginger . . ."

The amputation was disturbingly clean, not at all ragged like Kenny's had been. Bone and tissue peeked at him from the meat, making him think of raw chicken legs defrosting in a sink. Nash realized he was screaming louder than Ginger.

"Pull yourself together, Nash!" Felix bellowed. "Help me get her to shore!"

Felix pulled Ginger screaming on her back through the water, leaving Nash lagging behind, hanging on to her other arm. Ginger looked down, bewildered by her foot's absence, not fully comprehending what had just happened. She turned pale, moaning aloud, trying to gather the energy to scream again as the realization sank in. Nash's cries eclipsed hers.

"Felix! Here they come!"

The tiger was circling around for another attack, but the two white-tips it had been leading were now upon them. More commotion made it easy for the two smaller sharks to hone in and the spreading blood trail from Ginger's fresh wound was practically a runway to her flesh. The water was shallow, three feet, but the depth was no deterrent. The white-tips came rushing through the sea side by side, making their assault in unison. The first white-tip went low, crashing into Ginger's right calf from underneath. Her one foot kicked out and walloped it in the gills, discouraging the attack. Its teeth raked the skin of her thigh, but failed to find a grip before going wide.

The second white-tip was more on the mark, and far more determined. It broke the surface and went for Ginger's left side, the point of its nose ramming her ribs before its jaws clamped over her tiny love handle. Nash reached over and brought his fist down like a hammer on the shark's head. The white-tip held on, emboldened, shaking its head viciously as Ginger shrieked.

"Stab it!" Felix screamed. "Stab it, stab it, stab it!"

In his panic Nash had forgotten the weapon in his waistband. He snatched the dagger and raised it high above his head, pausing to target the monstrous snout. As he brought the dagger down the white-tip wrenched free a chunk of Ginger and pulled away. The wooden point missed the nose by inches, digging into Ginger's gaping wound instead.

"Aw, Christ, man," Felix wailed. "What the fuck are you doing?"

"F-f-fuck, I—I'm s-s-sorry," Nash stammered, wrenching the dagger out.

Blood gushed from her gored side, spreading through

the water in a trail that merged with the one flowing from her stump. Felix kept pulling, but Ginger's hand was limp in his grasp. What little energy she had left was being used to power her weakening screams.

"Not far now, girl!" Felix shouted. "You stay with us, y'hear? You're not allowed to die on me now!"

The tiger shark came fully around, racing inbound for a second helping, its fin and back high out of the shallow water. Felix grabbed his dagger and held it out. Nash copied, his breath coming in shaky gasps. He risked a glance at Felix.

"How do you suggest we stop this mother?"

Felix had no answer. The tiger rushed them, smashing Ginger with its flat nose and engulfing her hip and upper thigh in its maw. Both men brought their daggers down on its head. The skin was astonishingly thick, breaking off the tip of Nash's dagger before it sank an inch. Felix's strike did not fare much better. The shark jarred at the sting of the attack, but would not release. It wasn't leaving without another mouthful.

Felix wrenched his dagger out of the skin and brought it down again near the eye, sinking it deeper than before. The shark shook Ginger savagely, sounds of breaking bone and tearing skin filling the air. Felix managed one more stab and the shark pulled away, taking Ginger's footless leg with it and leaving a grotesque concave bite where her thigh once connected to her hip. Felix let out a cry of dismay and continued to pull Ginger toward the beach, Nash stumbling alongside. A white-tip fin rose quickly from the water on their right, blindsiding everyone, going unnoticed until it was upon them.

The first white-tip that had failed to get its pound of flesh rushed them defiantly in two feet of water. It lunged into Ginger's bleeding side, jaws pressed against her rib cage, teeth locked in. Ginger's cries hoarsened and withered. Felix released her and clasped his dagger in both hands, bringing it down hard on the flat of the shark's head, sinking the point deep. It let go and rolled, thrashing wildly, exposing its underside.

"Bitch!" he shrieked. "You goddamn *bitch*!"

Nash took over and pulled Ginger to shore, glancing back as Felix grabbed the shark by the tail and dragged it through the shallows. When the bitch was beached in less than a foot of water, Felix dropped to his knees with his dagger and stabbed furiously.

"We ain't so easy out of the water, are we?"

He struck again and again. The shark's thrashing subsided, jaws opening and closing uselessly on water and air. Over twenty blood-trickling puncture marks were left on the white belly before Felix was finished. Nash stared in disbelief as he pulled Ginger onto the beach. He didn't need to take her pulse to know she was already dead.

"Eat *that*!" roared Felix, pushing the twitching body

of the white-tip out to deeper water where the other sharks waited.

Felix waded ashore, staggering with each step. Nash sat on the sand, sick and stunned, still holding on to Ginger's hand. He caressed her flaccid fingers and looked over what remained. The missing leg was surreal. Nash was sure it had been the same one that cramped up on her. Intestinal tract spilled out of the hole in her side and coiled on the beach, where sand dusted it, resembling some hideous funnel cake.

"Ginger," Nash whispered, tears welling. "I'm so sorry."

Felix collapsed beside him, exhausted. He took one look at Ginger's evisceration and puked. Nash looked on as the injured white-tip was attacked in a frenzy of cannibalism. He could think of no worse fate in this world than being eaten alive.

Twenty-Four

He could think of no worse fate than being eaten alive, and Greer had seen much savagery in his life. He saw it as the pinnacle of pain, perhaps the greatest fear among all humans, to be consumed by something higher on the food chain while fully awake, aware that you were being separated and digested, reduced to nothing more than meat for a monster.

"I don't believe it," Turk said, climbing back aboard the yacht. "He actually wasted that white-tip."

Buchanan nodded as he secured the Zodiac to the stern. "That boy's got balls the size of goddamn grapefruits."

None of the four men applauded this time, although Felix's show of force was most deserving. Greer and Reposo stood watching the sharks attack the crippled member of their shiver in the shallows. Empty beer bottles littered the deck; an ashtray stuffed with the burned remnants of cigars lay in the middle of them. Buchanan negotiated the litter and lay back down on the deck with his M107. He used the scope to survey the spot where Nash and Felix sat.

"Get good footage?" Greer asked.

Buchanan grinned. "That junkie bitch just made the highlight reel."

Greer turned his attention to the survivors and waited. Felix and Nash did not move an inch. Buchanan redirected his scope to the commotion in the shallows where the sharks were finishing off the wounded white-tip. The white underside sank below the reddened waves. Circling fins followed it down.

"Didn't see that one coming," said Reposo. "Man beats shark."

"Four down, two to go," said Greer, lighting up another cigar. "You boys ready for the grand finale?"

"Hell yeah." Turk chuckled. "I gotta say how impressed I was this time. These folks were no disappointment—"

"Ah, shit."

They all turned to Buchanan, who was now pointing his M107 in a slightly different direction. Through the sniper scope he had seen something that no one else had. He glanced over his shoulder, at the cabin where the radio and radar were housed. Both of which hadn't been properly monitored in the last hour.

"Gentlemen," he said, "we may have a problem. . . ."

Twenty-Five

"We got a little problem. . . ."

Felix paused, gulping needed air. He took his eyes off the men on the boat just long enough to give Nash a look so unsettling that it made him shiver.

"I think they're just about done with us."

Nash believed it. They sat in silence, afraid to move in case it attracted any unwanted attention. Then something inside Nash reared its ugly head, making him twitch. He tried to ignore it, but it came again like a nervous tick.

"Shit."

"What's wrong?" Felix asked, but he already knew.

The first niggling for heroin buzzed Nash's brain stem, causing him to salivate. Drool escaped the corner of his mouth. He got to his feet, looking up and down the beach for the promised box. A thin, bare mast poked out over the top of the island's central vegetation, inviting investigation. He left Felix and what was left of Ginger and trudged up the beach to the grass and bushes for a better look. Three things came into view. The first two he expected, but not the third.

"Felix!" he yelled. "Get your ass over here!"

Felix rocked his bulk off the sand and came running. His eyes fell first on a small sailboat pulled ashore and the trunk nearby. Then he saw what had Nash so excited. About a mile out in the open water was a large cabin cruiser, headed in their direction.

"We're making a break for that boat," Felix said. "I ain't staying here to see what those psychos have in store for us."

Felix ran to the sailboat, casting a glance at the trunk on the sand as he passed. Nash followed, but stopped at the box and flipped open the lid. Everything Nash expected to see was inside, including a new white envelope. Nash grabbed it.

"Forget that," Felix barked. "We're not playing by their rules anymore."

Nash dropped the letter back into the box. "Fucking right we're not."

"Grab some of those water bottles and get in the boat," Felix said. "C'mon, make it quick now."

He paused, scratching a sudden prickly itch on his neck. Felix licked his dry lips at the thought of another snort of the delectable junk.

"Wait, grab the fucking dope too."

Nash grabbed an armful of water bottles and threw them into the hull of the boat, then went back for the metal container. He flipped up the lid to make sure. A full pound of dope lay within.

Shit, they weren't lying, Nash thought.

Nash looked again at the letter, suddenly tempted by its contents, intrigued by his tormentors' track record for telling the truth. If this was supposed to be the end of the game, what was left to tell?

. . . further instructions to retrieve something more for your troubles . . .

"Hey!" Felix yelled. "Pull your head out of your ass!"

Nash grabbed the letter again. "I think we should read this."

"Give me that."

Felix snatched the letter from Nash's hands, elbowing him out of the way for his disobedience. Felix was in charge now. There would be no democracy between two people, no more delaying decisions.

"I said *leave* it, Nash," he snarled, throwing the letter back in the box.

He grabbed Nash by the arm and pulled him stumbling toward the sailboat. They dragged the craft into the water, pointing the bow at the cabin cruiser off in the distance. Neither man knew a thing about sailing, but a pair of oars lay in the bottom of the boat. Rowing wasn't rocket science. Nash and Felix jumped in and each pegged an oar into a pivot. They dug the blades into the water and pulled, calling on strength they didn't even know they had. It wasn't long before Felix paused and gave Nash a nudge.

"I knew they wouldn't let us go that easily," Felix said, pointing.

The motor yacht was coming around the tip of the island at full speed. Felix rowed harder, urging Nash to do the same. He looked over his shoulder at the approaching cabin cruiser. Closer, but not nearly close enough.

"How far?" Nash wheezed.

Felix demanded that he double his efforts. Their tormentors were gaining fast. Nash stood in the boat and turned in the direction of the cabin cruiser, holding on to the mast for support. He leaned out, waving a hand frantically, trying to attract attention.

"Help!" he shouted. "Over here! *Help us!*"

A thunderclap rang out, echoing over the water. Nash heard a whistle of air a millisecond before the .50-caliber round blew through his outstretched hand, decimating it in a red mess of shredded fingers and busted bone. He watched the debris fly off the starboard side and pepper the water.

The thought came almost casually to his mind. *You'll never play the guitar again, Nash old boy.*

He didn't scream. He didn't even breathe. He simply stared at the remains of his hand floating on the waves.

"Nash!" Felix cried.

Nash sank to the gunwale, cradling his stump to his chest, his other arm slung around the mast. Blood spurted from his wrist, wetting his chest and running down his body into the bottom of the boat. Felix dropped to his knees, wrapping one big black arm around him and grabbing Nash's slack jaw in his hand.

"Stay with me, man," he ordered. "We come too far now."

Nash looked almost catatonic. Felix knew he was going into shock, so he did the only thing he could think of. He grabbed the container of heroin and dumped out a pile of powder into his palm.

"Here, buddy," he said. "Take a big sniff."

He crammed his palm up against Nash's nose. Nash inhaled, snorting and spluttering until he fell back with a giddy grin. His eyes went glassy over his dusted nostrils and lips as his burgeoning shock was temporarily sidelined.

Another thunderclap rang out, sending a second round splintering through the hull at the waterline and leaving a ragged hole the size of a softball through which water poured. Felix ducked, pulling Nash lower into the boat. A third shot sounded and exploded through the mast, showering Felix's side with sharp debris.

"Fuck you!" he screamed. "Fuck all of you!"

One more clap rang out, the shot whizzing harmlessly over the bow and into the water beyond. Quiet followed. Felix dared not even breathe. Wincing, he ran his fingers over the splinters embedded in his ribs. Dark blood surfaced around them and ran in thick trails down to his waistband. A minute passed before Felix dared to peek over the side of the boat. The yacht wasn't coming for them anymore. It had turned and was heading back around the island. Felix looked over his shoulder and let out a loud, mad cackle. The cabin cruiser, alerted by the sound of gunshots, was picking up speed. Felix figured it would arrive in less than ten minutes.

Bleeding profusely, he grabbed the oars with renewed vigor and pulled for safety, but their plight had worsened. His injuries, Nash rendered useless, and the fast-sinking sailboat tripled the difficulty. Blood and seawater washed around their ankles in the hull, rising quickly.

We're gonna sink long before that boat gets here, Felix thought.

He began to bail with cupped hands, but stopped when he realized their spilled blood would attract the sharks. They had even less time than he thought.

"Shit."

Felix watched his tormentors retreat farther while he tried his hardest to row faster, hoping to shorten the distance to the cabin cruiser as much as possible before the inevitable.

"How you doing down there, Nash? Are you still with me?"

Nash rolled his eyes up to Felix and raised his gored wrist so that they could both get a good look. Watery vomit came, a mash of swallowed salt water and food bits, spilling out over Nash's chin and onto his blood-ied chest.

"Christ, I hope I wake up anywhere but here," Nash said and passed out, crumpling to the thwart.

The first of the white-tipped fins appeared thirty yards off the starboard side, moving inquisitively toward the sailboat. Felix saw it approach and prepared himself.

"End of the line," he said.

Somewhere in the distance a gull cried out.

Twenty-Six

A gull cried out as Lieutenant Follson walked the length of the island in the early evening light. Ensign Parrish waited for him next to a trunk on the sand. Their coast guard cutter was moored off the north end of the island and Follson had just taken a dinghy ashore to examine further evidence of the day's insanity. He walked past two more of his men on the beach as they bagged what was left of a woman's body.

The trunk was now Follson's main focus. He pitied the poor sons of bitches whose sailboat had sunk out there and left them floating on the waves. The one who'd suffered the worst from the sharks was dead by the time he was pulled from the water. The other had somehow managed to survive the ordeal. Follson sincerely hoped the man would make a full recovery. The lieutenant had seen a lot in his years with the USCG, but nothing like this.

Parrish stood at attention and saluted the lieutenant as he approached.

"At ease, sailor. You touch anything, Parrish?"

"No, sir."

Follson stood over the open trunk and examined its contents. An envelope lying among the wrapped sandwiches and bottled water quickly attracted his attention. He snapped on a pair of latex gloves and pinched a corner between a thumb and finger.

"What is it, sir?" Parrish asked.

Follson lifted it out. "Do I look clairvoyant to you, Ensign?"

"No, sir."

Follson shook his head and smirked. Parrish was eighteen, four months into his service, and as green as they came. The boy could barely grow facial hair.

"You're standing in my light, Parrish."

Parrish shuffled to one side. "Sorry, sir."

Follson carefully opened the letter and held it out, allowing the setting sun to shine on the black typeface. He read the note aloud with great interest, enticing Parrish to come a step closer.

> *"Dear survivor,*
>
> *"Congratulations on completing our trials. If you have made it this far, you are deserving of more than just your heroin. At the opposite end of this island you will find a cross on the sand. Handsome compensation for your troubles is buried beneath it. A briefcase containing $50,000 cash, a cell phone, and a GPS receiver to aid in your rescue are waiting to be retrieved. We thank you for your participation."*

Lieutenant Follson folded the paper and looked to the opposite end of the island, his mind running the numbers, thinking through what he had just read. Parrish looked around, confused.

"What was going on here, sir?" he asked.

"Hell if I know, son."

"Fifty thousand dollars, Lieutenant? Cash? For real?"

There was a long pause as both men pictured that kind of money and the many things that could be bought with it.

"Go grab a shovel from the dinghy, Ensign," Follson ordered. "And don't breathe a word of this to the other men."

"Right away, sir."

"And double-time it, Parrish."

Parrish ran to where the dinghy was beached and grabbed an entrenching tool from the bow. He rejoined Follson, who led him farther down the beach to where he predicted the briefcase would be buried. In the fading evening light, they searched the long grass, growing excited at the prospect of finding buried treasure. It was a daydream that every sailor found himself indulging in at one point or another: coming across a pirate's trove of ill-gotten gains or a sunken Spanish galleon with gold in its belly. A buried briefcase with fifty grand was close enough.

"See anything, son?" Follson asked, growing impatient.

Parrish brushed back the long blades of grass and discovered a wooden cross jammed low into the sand.

"I think I found it, sir."

Follson knelt, examining the cross closely, considering options both legal and illegal. He had a duty to report his findings, but fifty thousand in cash could solve a lot of personal financial problems, and the USCG paid him a fraction of what he was worth for all his years of commendable service. After some consideration he turned to his subordinate, a crafty smile on his face. Parrish wasn't sure what it meant.

"What should we do, sir?"

"We should dig, Ensign."

"And what do we do if we find that money?"

"We keep it to ourselves. Are we clear?"

"Yes, sir."

Parrish began digging. As he shoveled he thought about all the sandbags he had filled back at base during his first few months. It had all been mere practice for this big payoff. When the hole was two feet deep he looked up at the lieutenant with excitement.

"There's definitely something down here, sir. And it looks like it's been buried fairly recently."

Follson leaned over the deepening hole, intrigued. Parrish kept digging. Finally the shovel connected with something hard. A metal ping emanated from just below the surface.

"Bingo—"

Both Follson and Parrish managed a second's worth of smile before the claymore mine detonated, tearing the muscle and tissue from their faces and shredding their bodies in an inverted hailstorm of shrapnel and sand.

Epilogue

When he awoke several nights later he couldn't recall his name. It was thirst that brought him around, parched tongue and sore throat begging for moisture. Weak and disoriented, he tried to rise. An ache that ran the length of his body stifled his movements, pain seeping from the very marrow of his bones. He lay still instead, nestled in a clean bed centered in a dark room, staring at the ceiling with blurry eyes. A night-light above his headboard illuminated him and little else. There was a window to his right, but only black beyond the glass. A closed door to his left revealed a single line of weak light at the base. Something behind his head beeped rhythmically, but a sharp pain in his neck forbade him to look. The air smelled of ammonia and bleach. It was the smell of a hospital.

"Hello?" he called.

No answer.

"Is anybody there?"

Still nothing, save the beeping. He had no memories to speak of, but broken, jagged thoughts began stabbing his head, angry at being shut out and eager to get back inside. For the moment he was glad to remember nothing. It felt like self-preservation. What he could not recall seemed better forgotten. He lay in silence, waiting while his eyes adjusted to the dark.

When he could see more clearly he began to inspect his surroundings. Only a bedside table with a clipboard atop was of interest. With much effort he reached over and snagged it. He brought the clipboard close to his face, eyes straining to see what was written. Printed in the top right-hand corner was the patient's name: Felix Fenton.

"God damn."

His voice trembled, withering and hoarse. Memories flooded back in, making Felix twitch. He experienced it all over again, every horrible instance. Salt water burned his throat; sand and rocks scraped his knees. Water beasts with skin like sandpaper came at him, teeth gnashing, tails thrashing, nictitating membranes rolling over eyes. Then blood came, blooming in a rolling underwater cloud before diffusing into shades of pink consumed by blue. The terrified faces of strangers who had quickly become comrades floated in and out of the thickest red, mouths open, screams drowning.

"I've escaped from hell. . . ."

There was a soft click and an open flame appeared in one of the dark corners of the room. It caught Felix by surprise, causing him to drop the clipboard to the floor with a clatter. A sitting figure was illuminated for a single moment before the flame died. The voice that came was gruff, unemotional.

"You're a hard man to kill, Mr. Fenton."

"Who's there? Where am I?"

The pungent smell of cigar wafted into Felix's nostrils. The heart monitor mounted on his bedpost quickened its rhythm. Motivated by fear, Felix found the strength to sit upright. In the corner, the cigar ember burned bright. Felix could make out a man's expressionless face in the pulsing orange glow. Even in the gloom something looked wrong with it, smooth where it shouldn't be, piebald in places. The eyes above were cold and piercing, shining as if made from polished marble. There seemed to be no irises in them, only pupils.

"You're in intensive care," Greer said.

"And who the fuck are you?"

"I'm the guy who helped put you here."

Somehow, Felix already knew. He looked around for something he could use as a weapon. There was an IV stand close by, the only thing within reach. He shifted toward it, but groaned at the pain that came with his effort. He tried calling for help instead.

"Doctor! Nurse!"

"No one is coming to your aid, Mr. Fenton. We have ensured this."

Felix tried again to move, succeeding only in breaking a sweat and increasing his discomfort. He risked another glance at the IV stand.

"Don't try to get up," Greer said, aware of Felix's intention.

Felix froze. He suddenly got the sense that there was more than just the one man in the room with him. He could feel other eyes watching him from the shadows.

"Why not?"

"Because all that's holding you together right now is thread and gauze."

Felix gently pulled back the sheets to examine his body. Much of his legs and body was wrapped in thick bandages. Both feet were in plaster casts. He tried to move them and felt the numerous sutures strain hot against the many wounds they were helping to keep closed.

"A hundred and thirty-six stitches in total," Greer continued. "Sharks kept a few pieces of you too, as a memento."

Felix gulped. "What did I lose?"

"Nothing that won't heal over time, except two toes

on your right foot and a good chunk out of your left calf. Your scars will sure be something special, but you've got enough meat on you to graft the worst of them."

Felix managed a middle finger. "Go fuck yourself."

A grunt came from elsewhere in the room, from someone else's throat. That was when Felix noticed the outlines of the other men standing perfectly still in the dark. One of them stepped forward and spoke. Felix recognized the voice, the Southern drawl of the man who had dropped him outside his apartment door.

"You best count your blessings while you can," Buchanan said. "It would be wise to show the captain here some respect."

Felix was taken aback. "Captain?"

Greer nodded, taking another drag on the cigar that seemed some sort of proboscis protruding from his mouth, ready to wound and cauterize on contact. Smoke drifted into his eyes, but he didn't blink. Felix knew the man wasn't being called Captain because he was a licensed mariner.

"You guys are military?"

"Formerly," Greer replied coolly. "Let's just say we're the kind of people that you meet only once, Mr. Fenton. For all intents and purposes, we're ghosts . . . technically we don't even exist."

Felix fell silent. The men surrounding his bed were

the best of the best gone rogue, and he was at their mercy. Then the realization sank in. If this privy information about his tormentors was being imparted to him, it probably meant that he was already dead. Felix figured he'd get some answers before the captain or one of his men put a bullet in his brain.

"Why?" Felix asked.

Greer snorted. "Why what?"

"Stranding us on an island. Baiting us with junk. Why would you do that to someone? Why us?"

"Because no one would miss you."

"And how do you know we wouldn't be missed?"

"Our contacts knew each of you well enough. They selected you and gave you up when we asked. They sold you out."

Felix wasn't following, but he didn't care to have Greer elaborate. There was only one question he wanted answered.

"Why did you do it?"

"You wouldn't understand."

"Try me."

Greer stared at him.

"I think I've earned some answers," Felix snapped.

Greer's face seemed to darken with anger, even in the shadows. "So far you've earned nothing from me other than a small show of mercy."

Felix didn't miss a beat. "And it's the *least* you could

do after what you put me through. Now, tell me why, God damn it."

There was a long pause. Greer took another drag on his cigar, thick smoke rolling out into the light as he exhaled. There was something about Felix he admired, a single man cornered by four others who could kill him in a heartbeat, and he was still demanding an answer to his question.

"I said you wouldn't understand."

"Humor me."

Greer's eye twitched. "Do you have any idea how most people feel about human excrement like you? How many folks sit behind the wheel of their car at a stoplight and cringe as you approach their windshield with a filthy rag and spray bottle? How many men see you passed out in a doorway or alley and for a moment hope you're dead? The number of women and children who see you hanging around their neighborhood one day and pray you won't be there the next? Do you have even the slightest inkling of how many people you come into contact with on a daily basis that would prefer if you somehow just disappeared overnight?"

Felix said nothing. If he were honest with himself, the numbers were staggering. He saw it in the eyes of so many he passed in the street day to day. Eyes of those on their way to work or school, eyes that told him he was garbage, viewing him as nothing more than disease and depravation. Those same eyes that sometimes said they'd rather see him a corpse in a gutter than the wandering urban zombie he'd become.

"Lack of conviction," Greer continued. "That's the only reason society doesn't go through with disposing of you. You're already dead from drugs and disease."

Greer's eye twitched again, pupil dilating and drifting. Felix didn't like it, a possible sign of growing instability in the man sitting before him.

"No, Mr. Fenton, what we did was help clean up Miami that little bit more. We simply made it more . . . sporting."

"Sporting?"

"Think of it as a kind of modern-day safari."

"You can go to Africa for that sort of shit, y'know."

Greer sighed. "I knew you wouldn't get it."

"Oh, I get it," Felix balked. "You guys are fucking psychopaths."

"Professional soldiers," Greer corrected. "There's a difference."

"Whatever. You're sick."

"We're sick?" Greer laughed. "Oh, that's rich coming from a junkie. Y'know what's truly sick? You, your kind, your neighborhood, your city, this whole damn country, addicted to anything and everything that can dull the pain for a minute. There's no supply without demand, and demand keeps rising. My men and I were

270

ordered to put our lives on the line again and again to help America win the war on drugs, to stem the flow of product that bankrolls those that wage war against us. I've been waist deep in more poppy fields than you can imagine, eradicated more cook houses than I can count. I built most of my career on exterminating or crippling the organizations you and your habits keep in business."

Greer's agitation grew, trigger finger stroking the air involuntarily as he remembered rounds unloaded into victims. He shifted in his seat, causing the chair legs to bang off floor tiles.

"And for what?" he continued. "We come home from war to find everyone strung out, more dope on the streets than ever before. Every enemy of this country sells us their poison by the boatload and we buy it faster than it can be brought to market. Afghan Brown, China White, Mexican Black Tar . . . our people want it all. Do you know how enraging that is for the patriots who pledge to protect this nation?"

Greer's rising anger worried Felix. He figured the climax of this speech was the precursor to his murder, a bullet or blade punctuating whatever point the captain was intent on making. He wondered which of the men would deliver it.

"Man, take it easy," Felix said, holding up a hand. "Don't go pinning your problems on me."

"My problem," Greer said with a grin, "is people like you."

Greer's smile terrified Felix, though he would not let it show. It looked as though it was carved into his face, exposed teeth and crescent lips whittled from knotted wood with crude blades. Felix expected blood to seep through those teeth at any moment, dribble down the mottled chin and onto the clean floor.

"And do you have any idea how big that problem is?" Greer continued. "No, you wouldn't, because you don't pay attention to anything outside your little bubble of eat, sleep, shit, and smack."

Greer leaned forward, shadows receding from him slightly. He raised a finger and tapped the side of his nose, letting one eyelid fall lazily over his pale blue iris in a horrible wink.

"See, I got to thinking. Maybe our enemies aren't the problem. Maybe the drugs aren't the problem. Maybe it's people like you that are the problem. You're the enemy."

"Me?"

Greer straightened, eyes blazing as he spoke, the cigar ember jutting out below seeming weak in comparison. "Take you and your demands off the table and everything else falls away."

Felix couldn't look at his tormentor anymore, but when he answered there was still enough grit in his voice to rub someone the wrong way.

"So . . . you round up a bunch of addicts and get your rocks off watching our pain and suffering? Is that it?"

"Your pain and suffering is self-inflicted, the by-products of the chemical pleasures you choose to indulge in to the detriment of yourselves and others. You can't even function as a normal human being anymore."

"And that makes me worthless?"

"Worse . . . it makes you hopeless."

Felix mouthed the word, unsure of how to respond. He had never felt more hopeless than at that moment, laid up in a hospital bed, injured and immobile, surrounded by a killer elite.

Greer blew smoke rings into the light. "It's clear to me that you and your kind ain't worth saving."

Felix gave him the hardest stare he could muster. "And that gives you the right to put me through all that nightmarish shit?"

"Why not?" Greer grinned, that festering cruelty showing in his mouth. "Tell me, Mr. Fenton, what else do you think a junkie parasite like you is good for?"

Felix looked down at his broken body. He had no idea what he was good for anymore. His usefulness ran out years ago, along with any aspiration other than attaining his next hit.

"I don't know," Felix admitted.

Greer stood and approached the bed slowly, one

hand behind his back. The more the light revealed him, the seared skin of his marred visage, the more Felix began to sweat. This was the hardest-looking man Felix had ever seen, and he'd fought some hard men in his time.

"I'll give credit where credit is due," Greer said. "You played the game better than anyone. You've got the kind of stones I can appreciate. For you, failure wasn't an option, was it? I've never seen anyone with so little to live for fight so hard to stay alive."

"You don't know what I live for," growled Felix.

Greer sneered. "But I know you're living at the moment. Which is more than can be said for your comrades, right?"

Felix looked up. "Nash didn't make it?"

"No one else made it. No one was *supposed* to make it. You're the lucky one."

"You call this lucky?" Felix seethed, striking the bed with a weak fist.

"You were given a fighting chance, which is more than we give most. Do you think Al Catraz will be so lucky the next time we set up a meeting with him?"

Felix's eyes widened. "You know Catraz?"

"We supply him with product. We've supplied a lot of people."

"And you're going to . . . kill him? I don't get it."

"He's been a dead man walking since we first made contact."

"Contact?"

"Every connection we make in the drug trade is allowed to live long enough to serve their purpose and help further our mission. We work from home now, play by our own rules, wage our own war. Catraz, and dealers like him, they unknowingly help us gather intel and infiltrate the networks, distributors, organizations that we target. When we have no more use for them, they're retired."

"Which is what you're about to do to me," Felix growled. "Go fuck yourself."

Greer didn't hesitate for a second, leaning in as he took the cigar from his mouth. He crushed the smoldering tip into the flesh of Felix's forearm and held it there against the screaming and writhing. The smell of burned meat mixed with that of the Cuban tobacco.

"You stupid shit," Greer hissed. "I'd have smothered you in your sleep if I wanted you dead. You really, really don't know how good you've got it right now, do you?"

Greer held it for another second then threw the crumpled cigar away. Felix's wails wound down, threatening to turn into sobs. He held back the tears as Greer walked around the bed to where the IV bag hung and prodded the clear plastic bag with a finger.

"You know what they got you on? You're pumped full of OxyContin. That's some of the best shit they got to help you junkies kick the habit. I'd say you've fallen ass backward into a good thing here, the best rehabilitation money can buy."

"Yeah, until they realize I can't pay," Felix moaned. "Soon as that happens they'll disconnect me and toss my ass out on the street."

"That won't happen," Greer replied. "We're the ones footing your bill, and we're going to continue to pay it until you're fully recovered."

"Why would you do that?"

"Because we think you've earned it, Mr. Fenton. You are the exception."

Greer paused, an unexpected emotion creeping into his face. Felix wouldn't have thought it possible, but for one brief moment the captain appeared to sadden. He let out a long, aggravated breath and continued.

"Things didn't end the way we planned this time."

"You mean because I didn't die?"

"Among other things," Greer said. "There was collateral damage, unforeseen and unfortunate, when the coast guard came to investigate the aftermath of your ordeal and tried to locate your money."

"Money? What money?"

"The money we lied about in the letter that you never read. It was a smart move on your part to ignore our last note, Felix, because we were betting on your greed and need for the grand finale. We proposed a hell of a payday, something that would end everything with a bang. Even good men in the service succumbed to the temptation."

One of the other men stepped from the shadows and handed Greer something rectangular in the gloom. Greer held it up to the light, showing off the black briefcase. He unlocked the latches and opened it to reveal stacks of money inside.

"Fifty thousand dollars," Greer said. "More than enough money to start over."

He closed the case with a snap.

"Or enough cash to keep you supplied with smack for a good while."

Greer placed the case at the foot of the bed and took a step back into the dark. Felix stared at the case that contained more money than he'd ever hoped to see at one time. He thought about what that money could buy. The dreams he could fulfill were endless, but that quantity of cash could score the kind of highs he'd only ever hoped to afford.

The sliding click of metal on metal came, the unmistakable sound of a round being chambered. Greer stepped forward into the light, .45 automatic held out before him and pointed at Felix's head. Felix tried to scoot backward, bobbing his head away from the gun's line of fire until he banged it against the headboard. The beep of the heart monitor began to gallop. Greer kept coming until he pushed the cold steel barrel up against Felix's right eye. The smell of gun oil chased away that of the cigar.

"W-w-what are you doing?" Felix stammered.

Greer's words slid through clenched teeth. "You of all people should appreciate the second chance you've got here. I don't know what you're going to do when you get out, Felix Fenton, but know that I'll be keeping tabs on you. And if I think you haven't gotten my point, rest assured that I'll do you in before the heroin does. Understand?"

Felix's nod was little more than a tremble. He sat rigid, every muscle in his body stringent, anticipating the gun to go off and splatter the last of his frantic thoughts over the wall behind him. Too soon this terror was being visited upon him. He thought his damaged body might give out. His head felt compressed, dry throat bouncing his Adam's apple, teeth grinding, one brown eye squinted against the muzzle of the gun. His heart hammered, pumping blood through weak flesh. Trickles of sweat ran from his temple. Greer pushed the gun harder into Felix's eye before pulling it back and gently releasing the hammer with his thumb.

"Don't test me."

Greer backed away into the shadows, his men gathering around him. Felix closed his eyes and whispered a prayer of sorts, thanking whatever may have been watching over him for staving off death once more. Shuffling sounds and the soft click of a door being closed came to his ears. By the time Felix dared to look again the room was empty.

Felix breathed deep and listened to his heart monitor. The beeping began to smooth out. He regarded the case of money at his feet, his bandaged body, the needle scars on both his arms. He weighed his options, wondering how long he could stay clean if he tried and how well he could disappear with the cash if he didn't. Nine out of ten addicts never recover. Felix never liked those odds.

Acknowledgments

I owe a heartfelt thanks to my family: my father, Tony, my mother, Angela, and my sister, Emma. Your love, support, and influence are immeasurable.

To Dr. Dominik Zbogar for putting up with me and never letting me down.

To Peter Sellers for always setting the bar just out of reach.

To Annabel Merullo, Rachel Mills, Laura Williams, and all the incredible people at Peters, Fraser, & Dunlop.

To my excellent editors, Denise Roy and Adrienne Kerr, and the great folks at Plume.

Last, but not least, to Kara for having the utmost faith in my abilities, especially when I don't. She knows things long before I do.

He just wanted a decent book to read ...

Not too much to ask, is it? It was in 1935 when Allen Lane, Managing Director of Bodley Head Publishers, stood on a platform at Exeter railway station looking for something good to read on his journey back to London. His choice was limited to popular magazines and poor-quality paperbacks – the same choice faced every day by the vast majority of readers, few of whom could afford hardbacks. Lane's disappointment and subsequent anger at the range of books generally available led him to found a company – and change the world.

'We believed in the existence in this country of a vast reading public for intelligent books at a low price, and staked everything on it'
Sir Allen Lane, 1902–1970, founder of Penguin Books

The quality paperback had arrived – and not just in bookshops. Lane was adamant that his Penguins should appear in chain stores and tobacconists, and should cost no more than a packet of cigarettes.

Reading habits (and cigarette prices) have changed since 1935, but Penguin still believes in publishing the best books for everybody to enjoy. We still believe that good design costs no more than bad design, and we still believe that quality books published passionately and responsibly make the world a better place.

So wherever you see the little bird – whether it's on a piece of prize-winning literary fiction or a celebrity autobiography, political tour de force or historical masterpiece, a serial-killer thriller, reference book, world classic or a piece of pure escapism – you can bet that it represents the very best that the genre has to offer.

Whatever you like to read – trust Penguin.

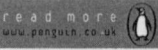